LOSING PRINCETON CHARMING

C.M. SEABROOK

FRANKIE LOVE

Copyright © 2019 by C.M. Seabrook

All rights reserved.

No part of this book may be reproduced in any form or by any electronic or mechanical means, including information storage and retrieval systems, without written permission from the author, except for the use of brief quotations in a book review.

LOSING PRINCETON CHARMING

All is fair in love and war ... but is this love?

Spencer Beckett may have fallen hard for Charlotte Hayes, but one lie has their relationship crashing to the ground.

Their glass castle is about to shatter. Breaking Spencer's heart in the process.

When tragedy strikes, Charlie needs a man who won't let her down.

Even princes need second chances ... but there's still a knight fighting for her honor, asking for her hand.

Who will be there when she needs saving?

And what happens if she tries to save herself?

One kiss and Spencer knew: it was Charlotte, always Charlotte.

He isn't quitting on her. Not now. Not ever.

One day his princess will come.

1

CHARLIE

THERE ARE moments in your life that you know as they're happening will change everything. The sting of Tatum's fist against my temple, the sharp crack as it hits, even through the shock of it and the nausea that builds, I know the damage is irreversible. And that everything is about to change.

Oh god. I suck in a breath, bile rising in my throat, and try to keep the damp towel from sliding off my body as my knees give out on me.

Tatum drops beside me, "Charlie, shit. I didn't mean...fuck..."

"Get away from her." Spencer pushes Tatum away, and even though the man is a good three inches taller and twenty pounds bigger, he lets him.

"I'm...okay," I manage to say, despite the throbbing in my temple. I know Tatum didn't mean to hurt me, but Spencer is looking for any excuse to push my best friend aside.

"Get some fucking ice," Spencer spits out, lifting me in his arms. Anger vibrates off him, intense, cold, his features like stone. And I know what he thinks, what it looks like - me being here at Tatum's place, practically naked. But I'd needed my best friend, needed the warmth of alcohol to dull the pain of having Winslow Harrington humiliate me, knowing Spencer was what? Too embarrassed to invite me to the benefit.

He'd lied to me, and yet right now it's me who feels like I have to justify my actions.

"Spencer, it's not what you think...nothing happened..."

His jaw clenches, lips thin and he doesn't look in my eyes. But he also doesn't release me, just picks me up and carries me to the living room and sits me down on the couch.

When Tatum returns with a washcloth filled with ice, Spencer places it on my temple. The ice burns when it touches my skin, but I know it's necessary. I can practically feel a bruise forming.

"Is she okay?" Tatum asks. "Should I call an ambulance."

"No," I groan out, trying to push away from Spencer, but the world spins. "Oh, god, I feel...sick..."

It's only partly because I just had the wind knocked out of me...and it's not the whiskey either. It's being here, naked, only a towel around me. I know how this looks. Doesn't matter how much Spencer trusts me, this is bad. I can only imagine how I'd feel if the situation was reversed.

"I'm sorry," I mutter, closing my eyes as another wave of dizziness hits me.

"Where the fuck are her clothes?" Spencer's voice is low, hard, filled with venom. I've never felt his wrath before, but even though he won't meet my gaze, I can feel all his anger - his hurt.

"She puked on them." Tatum sounds utterly miserable, and when I glance over, I catch his eyes before he looks away, guilt tightening his features. "I put them in the wash."

"Get her something to wear. Now." The last word is a demand that has even me jumping slightly.

Tatum leaves again, but I wish I could reach out and pull him into a hug, let him know that *I know* this was an accident - but I'm still naked and

Spencer is here, and it's not the time to comfort him.

Spencer's right eye twitches. "This is so fucked up."

My gaze narrows on him. And while I agree with his statement, and even though my temple throbs I can still read the man who lied to me - he's hiding something. I saw him at the auction. If he wants to get all high and mighty with me now, he has another thing coming.

I'm not the one who has been keeping secrets.

"Here." Tatum is back, and he places a hoodie and sweats on the coffee table beside the empty bottle of Jameson.

I groan when I see it. "No more whiskey...ever again."

Spencer just grunts as he helps me sit up, then hands me the hoodie, glaring at Tatum.

"I'll, uh...go. Let you change," Tatum says, starting to turn toward his bedroom. "I'm really sorry, Charlie."

"I know." I hold the ice to my head. "It was an accident."

He swallows hard and nods before disappearing into his room. The shot was meant for Spencer, and if I hadn't stepped between them, it would have been him with a raging headache right now. But the cut on Spencer's swollen bottom lip makes me think he was already fighting before he got here.

"What happened?" I reach out to touch his face and he flinches.

"Prescott," he says icily, eyes narrowing but still not meeting mine, and I know not to press him. He helps me dress, tension and anger pouring off him with each movement. "Can you walk?"

"Yeah. I think so..."

He takes my elbow and helps me stand. "Then let's go."

I frown at him. "Where?"

"My place."

"So you believe me?" I hate that my words are still slurred, but not even throwing up or being clipped in the temple by Tatum could get rid of the buzz of half a bottle of whiskey. "That nothing happened with—"

Spencer stops and finally meets my gaze. His eyes are so damn cold, hard. I've never seen him look at me that way before. Like he barely knows me. Like he doesn't trust me.

"I don't know what the hell to believe. But I'm not leaving you here."

I swallow, placing my hands on his chest. His

bowtie hangs haphazardly around his neck and there are specks of blood on his white button-down, and I realize that his tuxedo jacket is missing. His hair sticks up at odd angles like he's been tugging at it, and when I hold his gaze, his eyes look almost haunted. But even worse, I see the accusation there, the betrayal.

My chest squeezes painfully. "I'd never cheat on you, Spencer."

He pinches the bridge of his nose and takes a few steadying breaths. "Let's just go. We can talk about this tomorrow when you're not drunk."

"I'm not—"

His hard gaze stops my protest.

I don't say anything else until we're back at his place. But the silence has infused my own frustration. I get why he's upset. What it looked like when he walked in. But I wouldn't have been with Tatum in the first place if Spencer had just told me the truth about the party.

And then there was Winslow, flaunting her position, her status in front of me. In the past, I'd never have let someone like her make me feel less than. But I know now there's this secret part of me that wants to be more, wants to be someone who Spencer can be proud of. And I know after tonight that I'll never be that person, for one reason only - I wasn't born with a silver spoon in my mouth.

"Let me see," Spencer says when we're in his kitchen. He takes the ice pack from me and gently runs his fingers over my temple. "You're going to have a bruise, but it doesn't look too bad."

I place my palm over his hand, needing his touch, the reassurance of it.

When did I become this girl?

Locked in a silent exchange, I see all the words he wants to say flash in the cold blue depths.

"Let me explain, Spencer."

He gives a hard shake of his head and drops his hand, then starts to walk out of the room. "In the morning."

I follow him up the stairs to his bedroom, watching as he starts to undress.

God, he's beautiful. And cold. And distant. Nothing like the playful Princeton Charming I've come to know and love...yes, *love*. I'm falling in love with him. Or maybe I've been in love with him this whole time.

But tonight, love doesn't change the fact that I will never be accepted by his family and friends. That there will always be people like Winslow

Harrington trying to break us up, and making sure I know my place.

That's why all this started. Why I called Tatum in the first place. Spencer still doesn't know about the stunt his ex-girlfriend pulled. How she tried to humiliate me in front of his parents and peers. Or that I saw him there, that I know he lied to me about where he was going tonight.

"Spencer, I was at the—"

"I said we'll talk in the morning." He slams his phone and wallet on the dresser.

"If you'd just listen."

He turns and pins me with a look that makes me suck in a breath. "I'm trying really fucking hard to stay calm, Charlie. But I'm pissed. And if we do this now..." He rubs the back of his neck and looks up at the ceiling. "I know I'm going to say things I'll regret. So do me this one favor and go to sleep."

I inhale a shaky breath and give a small nod, even though there's a part of me that wants to fight, that needs to say the things that are bottled up. But my thoughts are still fuzzy, and I know I'll lose any argument we have. So I stand there and watch him, unsure what to do. It would be better if I just called an Uber and went back to my dorm.

When he's just in his boxer briefs, Spencer

tosses the comforter aside and gets into bed then turns the light off.

A few seconds pass before I make the decision to crawl in next to him. I feel like crap. My stomach still churns and my head throbs. Worst, my emotions are a confused mess.

I want him to hold me, to pull me to his side, but he doesn't, and we lay there in silence. My heart breaking. My chest squeezing painfully with all the things I want to say.

I. Love. Him.

Three words we've never said to each other. But I do. I love him and need him, and at the same time, there's a piece of me that wishes I'd never met him.

How fucked up is that?

"I care about you, Spencer," I say into the darkness, knowing things between us are irreparably broken, and not liking the person I've become lately.

Anxious.

Needy.

Insecure.

"Don't say anything else tonight, Charlie." It's a warning, one I know I should listen to.

But I don't. My mom always said my stubbornness would get me into trouble, and I know right now she's right. Still, I can't stop myself. I need to get things off my chest. And yeah, I'm still feeling the effects of the whiskey. I'm emotional, close to tears, and yet numb at the same time. And all I want is for him to pull me against his chest and tell me everything will be all right, and yet hating myself for how much I want it even after he's hurt me - *after I hurt him.*

"I think..." *If you just hold me, maybe I'll believe everything will be okay, that we'll be okay.* I want to say the words, but instead, I say coldly. "I wasn't the only one who made mistakes tonight."

He huffs out a hard breath. "Go to sleep."

I roll over on my side, my back to him, clutching a pillow against my chest, a single tear rolling down my cheek.

Why does it feel like my world is unraveling? *Because you're drunk*, that rational voice says in my head. Too bad my tongue doesn't listen.

"I want to be with you...but..."

Spencer's breathing is heavy, and he says tightly, "But what?"

Don't say it. Don't say it.

"I just...I don't think this thing between us is going to work."

He's silent for a long moment before he finally says roughly, "Yeah, Charlie. I think you might be right."

I hear the truth in his voice - I'm losing Princeton Charming. And as much as it hurts, I wonder if it's not for the best.

2

SPENCER

As hard as I tried, I didn't sleep a minute last night, so as soon as the sun rises I get out of bed and go for a run, needing the frigid air and the rush of adrenaline to clear my head.

I don't know what to feel. Anger, frustration, betrayal, they swirl through me like a goddamn vortex, demanding that I end things with Charlie.

I'd felt like a fucking ass putting the tracker on her phone, some primal part of me claiming that it was for her own protection. But I know it's because I'd let Prescott get into my head. I didn't trust her. Not completely. And I'd used it to track her down last night when she wasn't answering my calls.

Because I knew something was wrong. Could feel it in my bones. But nothing had prepared me for walking into Tatum's apartment and seeing my girlfriend coming out of the shower - naked in another man's apartment.

Doesn't matter how much she had to drink, there's no excuse, nothing she can say to make this better.

Maybe nothing happened. But the fact that she put herself in a compromising position, that she turned to Tatum for whatever was eating at her, it's just another wedge between us. And the world has already placed enough of them between us.

My lungs are burning as I walk through the front door, expecting to find Charlie still asleep, but she's in the kitchen, making a pot of coffee, still dressed in Tatum's fucking clothes.

"You're awake," I say gruffly making her jump.

"Oh, hi." She turns, chewing nervously on her bottom lip, her phone in hand. Her hair is a mess, and there are dark circles under her eyes, a purple bruise on her temple, but her shoes are on. She's itching to go.

I have to clench my hands into fists to keep from reaching out for her, from pulling her into my arms. All night I struggled to keep to my side of the bed. But I knew what would happen if I didn't. I wouldn't be able to stop myself from taking her, consuming her...claiming her.

"Feeling better?" I ask.

"Barely." She runs a hand through her tousled hair. "I'm never drinking again."

I manage a small smile, but god it's painful. The thought of her naked with Tatum is punishment enough for lying to her.

But I know she won't see it that way.

"Look," she says. "I know we said we'd talk today, but my boss called to check in on me. There's an extra shift I can pick up this morning and so I'm going to head back to the dorm to change so I can make it in time."

My eyes widen. "You're going to leave without finishing this conversation?"

"I was willing to have it last night but you—"

I cut her off. "I'm sorry. You're right. I'm sleep deprived and the last thing I want is to fight with you."

"You mean that?" she asks, frowning, searching my gaze.

I step toward her, taking her hand in mine. "I do."

Her pouty lips twist, but there is a glimmer of relief in her eye. "Good because I don't want to fight with you either. I know we have stuff to figure out, but maybe it would be better after we've had time to cool down?"

"Agreed." I take hold of both her hands, our fingers lacing.

Her words last night still echo in my head. *I don't think this thing between us is going to work.* I'd told her that she was probably right, but god those words had cut deep.

"I don't want to lose you, Charlie. Not over—"

She lifts an eyebrow. "I thought the conversation was on hold?"

"Right, sorry." I chuckle, running my hand over her hair, and breathing her in. "God, you look cute with bedhead."

"You are such a dork, Spencer Beckett." Her words are playful, but I know it's a front. Her way of making all of this less painful.

"Yeah, but I'm your dork." I wink and lean closer, needing this - needing her.

The corners of her mouth turn down, gaze searching. "You mean that?"

I nod, wishing it could be this simple. Wanting it to be, even if it's impossible. Taking a risk, I ask, "Can I take you out after work?"

She frowns. "I have that poli-sci test on Tuesday. I've got to study."

"We can meet at the library? I know a quiet corner where we can get cozy."

She shakes her head. "Not cozy. We need a spot where we can focus and talk."

"Yeah, you're right." Truth is, I want to focus on her without anyone or anything dividing my attention. "I've got a perfect spot on the third floor. I'll bring take-out and we can make a night of it."

"Take-out in the library? That's against like a hundred rules."

I chuckle. "I've never been one to play by the rules."

Instead of laughing like she'd usually do, my comment makes her frown. "I have to go."

I check her out as she turns to grab her purse, even in another man's sweats she is undeniably beautiful. I know she needs to get to work, but damn, I'd kill to pull her into my bed and fall asleep with her in my arms. After we kissed and made up first, of course.

"See you at four?" I ask as she pulls open my front door.

She gives me a small smile. "It's a date."

Needing to clear my head, I decide to go for a second run after Charlie leaves. I know I won't fall back asleep - not now and I'm a glutton for punishment. I'm buzzing with adrenaline and have nothing to do with it. So instead I pull on my running shoes and pop in my earbuds.

Cheesy, maybe, but I put on the playlist Charlie sent me a few days ago of some of her favorite songs. Many of them are familiar, and I actually find myself relaxing by the time I push through mile five.

Last night was a disaster on so many levels. Finding Charlie the way I did for starters. But also my fight with Prescott. The words I shouted at my father.

All of it brings me to one conclusion, I need to know what I really want before I make any drastic decisions.

But damn, I'm a selfish prick for wanting Charlie to be by my side as I figure my shit out. I knew I wasn't good enough for her, and now I feel that way twenty-fold. I just made plans with her again, knowing I'm the last thing she really needs.

I slow to a jog as I finish my work out, suddenly

famished. My stomach is growling, considering a donut and coffee. I'm just turning back toward my place when I bump into Charlie's friend Jill. She's out running too, and she waves hello.

I stop, catching my breath. "Hey," I say, both of us pulling out our earbuds. "How's it going?"

She groans, clutching her sides. "God I hate running," she says. "But it's better than dieting."

She has bright blue eyes and is nearly six foot tall. Charlie has told me they bonded over campus jobs and she was there for me before Christmas when I couldn't get a hold of Charlie. I know she is someone I can trust, and right now, considering I'm not exactly getting on famously with Charlie's other best friend, I could use this time to my advantage.

I laugh, pointing to the donut shop across the street. "That's where I was headed. Want to join me?"

She shrugs. "I mean, I did just run two miles, that's practically a thousand free calories, right?"

"I'm not counting," I say as we cross the street. As I push open the doors of the donut shop, sugar floods the senses. "God, I'm starving."

Jill grins. "Didn't make Charlie breakfast in bed today? What kind of man are you?"

I scratch the back of my head, not wanting to

get into it. "She took a shift this morning so she left early."

"Ah, okay then. Glad to hear she's feeling better. Heard she left the catering gig early last night because she wasn't feeling well."

"Right," I say, faking that I know anything about Charlie cutting out of work. What else didn't she tell me about last night? "She was fine this morning."

We place our orders, then take our coffee and donuts to a small table in the corner.

"So, I need your help with a date," I say. I know that it's just a study date, but I have a lot of mileage to make up for. Yes, she was with Tatum, but before that, I was at a party I didn't invite her to.

Sure, I was doing it for her own good - our own good - but I'm no fool. I can see it was a dumbass decision. Hindsight is twenty-twenty, and all that.

"What kind of date?" Jill asks as she breaks her old fashioned in half.

"I have a study date with Charlie tonight. She's prepping for a test. And I want it to be..." I shrug. "Perfect."

Jill laughs. "And where will this study date take place?"

"The Princeton Library."

She moves her eyebrows up and down. "Nothing says sexy like college textbooks."

I chuckle, knowing it isn't the most romantic location. But right now I don't need to shower Charlie with romance, we just need to try and find some common ground. We need to figure out if we can make this relationship, or whatever is left of it, work.

"I know, I know," I say. "But what are some of her favorite things? You guys are close, right?"

"Yeah, but aren't you the one dating her?"

I take a bite of my donut. "Yeah, but when we are together, everything is really...charged. We still have a lot to learn about one another."

"And you want to make her swoon?" Jill asks, grinning.

"Pretty much."

"Then you need to get good snacks. We're talking popcorn. Gummy worms. And Diet Dr. Pepper."

I laugh. "You sure? I've never seen Charlie drink soda."

Jill shrugs. "Have you ever crammed for a test with her? Oh, and index cards. And highlighters. And Post-it notes. She takes test prep as seriously as she took the SATs."

"Were you friends with her back in high school?"

Jill shakes her head. "No, but I do know she didn't have a tutor and still got a near perfect score."

I nod, impressed. I knew Charlie was smart, that she worked her ass off to get into Princeton, but I guess I didn't realize just how passionate she was about her education.

"When it comes to school, she doesn't mess around," Jill says. "That's why getting into the master's program means so much to her."

"I admire that so much. Her work ethic is impressive. My father's colleagues could learn something from her playbook."

Jill finishes her donut and points a finger at me. "Yeah, Charlie is a special person. It's why you better not hurt her."

I frown. "I'm not planning on it." But I know just being around me it's going to happen. People are cruel, especially over-privileged assholes who think they're better than people whose wallets aren't overflowing with old money.

Jill leans back in her chair, watching me. "Your intentions seem good, but she deserves a man who will stick by her side, through thick and thin. Not just because she's pretty."

"What are you saying?" I narrow my eyes at her.

"That you're Princeton Charming for a reason, and Charlie is...well, she's a sweetheart. I don't want to see her get hurt."

"Duly noted," I say, trying to push away my frustration. Jill isn't even giving me the benefit of the doubt. But then again, I have a reputation for a reason. I don't want to be that man when I'm with Charlie. I want to be...better.

Jill is frowning at me now. "I know you didn't write those blog posts or whatever, but whoever did should pay. No one deserves that."

"I couldn't agree more. Charlie deserves the whole fucking world."

She smiles then. "Good, glad we're on the same page, Mr. Beckett."

I chuckle. "Didn't realize grabbing donuts with you meant getting the third degree."

Standing to go, Jill says, "Don't worry, you passed the test."

But will I pass Charlie's?

We say goodbye, and I try to squelch the uneasiness I feel. The donuts didn't seem to take care of the pit in my stomach.

Truth is, Jill's words hit home. Charlie deserves everything - and after last night I wonder if I am the man who can give it to her.

3

CHARLIE

When I get to the library, I text Spencer.

Me: Where is this cozy corner you promised?

Spencer: Third floor. Past Greek mythology. To the right.

After a long shower, and an even longer shift, I am looking forward to sitting down with a pile of books and notes and losing myself in school work. Having some eye-candy won't hurt, but I am really hoping Spencer will be more of a help than a distraction. To be honest, all day I've been wrestling with what to do with him, where this relationship should go. Deep down I think I know what needs to happen, but I'm not ready to admit it. I don't want to face the truth about Spencer and me, because when we're together, everything clicks.

And maybe that's enough.

Regardless, I do know that this poli-sci test isn't going to study itself. As I climb the second flight of stairs, I follow his instructions, without much expectation. If things don't go well between us, I can always head back to my dorm and study there.

But when I find him sitting on a leather couch in a corner, just as he promised, my eyes widen. "You did all this?" I ask, taking in the goodies he has set out on a table.

"I tried to get your favorites."

"How did you know I crave Diet Dr. Pepper when I am in full on study mode?" I ask, dropping my bag and peeling off my layers. It is still freezing outside, and I place my gloves and hat on top of my coat.

"I may have asked a friend."

I smile. "Well whoever it is, they know me well. This is impressive." He has a pile of index cards and a jar of pencils and highlighters. Along with a dry erase board on an easel. "Are we going to get in trouble for setting up camp like this?"

Spencer shakes his head. "Being Princeton royalty has its privileges."

I laugh, settling in next to him. "Thank you," I say, touched by his thoughtfulness. "This was really sweet."

"I know we have things to talk through, but tonight, let's just focus on this test, okay?"

I smile, appreciating that he isn't pressuring me for answers right now - answers I'm guessing neither of us really want to say aloud.

"So, what chapter are we focusing on?" he asks, taking the book from my hands.

I reach for a handful of popcorn, knowing that this - being here, cozy with Spencer, is the only place I want to be right now.

Maybe it's my way to avoid reality - the hard conversation I know we have to face eventually.

But right now, avoidance feels really, really good.

Hours later the cozy nook is a disaster zone. Empty cans of soda litter the table, there is a half-empty bowl of popcorn, and we are both half asleep. And the lights to the library have all turned off, except for our little corner. Spencer must have seriously pulled some strings.

"I think the library is closed," I say. "Maybe we should call it a night."

"How about I quiz you one more time?" he asks, sitting up straighter.

"Okay, but this time we make it a game."

"What kind of game?"

I bite the corner of my mouth, wanting to thank Spencer properly for being such a good sport tonight. "Is there such thing as a Strip-Quiz?"

His brows go up. "It can be now."

I snort. "You are such a boy."

He lifts a finger. "I'm pretty sure this game was your idea."

"Good point," I say, laughing. "Okay here are the rules. Every time we get an answer wrong we have to remove an item of clothing."

Spencer grunts in approval. "How about we cut to the chase and just fuck like I know we both want?"

My cheeks burn. "I had no idea studying turns you on so much," I tease.

"It's you who turns me on, Charlie Hayes. You alone."

He leans over and kisses me then, his mouth on mine sending a thousand pricks of desire over my body. His lips are soft, and his tongue finds mine.

It's like he is exploring me for the first time all over again.

"Oh Spence," I whisper, wanting this. Him. So bad. I pull him on top of me, unbuckling his pants as I do. Being here, in a public place, feels forbidden and exciting. The rush of doing this with him here makes me giddy.

"I like the whole naughty schoolgirl thing," he tells me, pushing down my leggings, his hand on my wet pussy. God, he gets me so ready, so freaking fast.

"Sorry I don't have on knee socks or a plaid skirt."

"You don't need that shit."

I wrap my fingers around his shaft, his thick pulsing cock getting me so wound up. "No?" I ask. "You don't have a fantasy of a woman in costume?"

"I prefer you naked, under me. I don't need any accessories. Just my cock and your sweet pussy."

"And I'm the naughty one?" I ask with a laugh.

"God, you feel so good, Charlie," he says as he guides his length inside of me. I moan, wrapping my arms around his neck as he begins to fill me up. My body is humming with pleasure as he moves inside of me.

It's fast, the way my body opens for him, like his

thickness inside of me was the one thing I've been missing all this time.

"I love fucking you," he tells me as he moves deeper inside me.

I gasp, my fingers digging in his hair, holding on to him as he thrusts hard and fast inside me.

As he is just finishing, I hear a noise behind us. A click of a camera.

"What the fuck?" Spence shouts, pulling away from me. I feel exposed, but as I look in his eyes, I know he does too.

He moves toward the noise, and I pull up my pants.

There's a commotion, Spencer swearing, and I see a dark figure move in the shadows, their identity hidden by a black hoodie. Books fall off shelves as Spencer goes after them. But they're too quick. The only good thing is that they dropped their phone, which Spencer retrieves.

"What the fuck?" His anger pulses off of him, and it's not an overreaction. I feel shook up and stunned. "This place is supposed to be locked up, except for the security guard."

"Maybe it was the blogger? Trying to…" Tears fill my eyes. It's all too much. If those photos got out…if my parents saw...

Spencer grips the phone, fingers whitening around it. "I'll give this to my guys, maybe they can trace it."

"Delete the photos first, Spence, I don't want anyone to see...anyone to think..."

He nods, touching the screen of the smartphone. "It's locked. But I'll break into it. Or I will find someone I trust implicitly to help."

"Thanks," I say with a shaky breath. "Kind of ruined the mood."

Spencer nods, his jaw tight, his eyes dark. "Maybe after I call security, it's time we have the conversation we've been avoiding."

I wipe the tears from my eyes. Not wanting this, but also knowing it's inevitable.

And after what just happened, it's imperative. It's not just Spencer's reputation on the line. It's mine too.

4

SPENCER

After I speak with my security guys, Charlie and I clean up the area where we spent all evening. The mood is dark, tainted by the fucking asshole who tried to cash in on our relationship.

I didn't get a good look at them. With the rush of adrenaline, me trying to pull my pants up and chase after them, not to mention the shadows and the hoodie that covered their face, I don't even know if the intruder was a guy or a girl. All I know is that when I do find out their identity, they better have a good fucking lawyer.

"Come on, let's get you in your coat," I say, helping Charlie get bundled up.

She's still shaken up, and I don't blame her. I should never have let things get so heated up in a public place. Even if I thought we were alone. One thing my parents did teach me is that there's always someone watching.

We walk down the steps of the library, words hanging between us. The conversation we both want to avoid heavy around us. But it won't help either of us to not get it all out in the open.

Even if it's going to hurt like hell.

In my car, I turn on the ignition, warming it up. I want to take her hand in mine again, pull her to me. But every time I do, it leads to sex.

And sex isn't going to fix what's broken between us. And that's the truth of it...Charlie and I are broken. *I'm* broken. But I'm not sure who the hell I am without her. I just know I have to find out. For her sake and for my own.

The ache in my chest turns sharp when the thought goes through my head.

Because I want her still.

I think I...fuck...I'm pretty sure I'm in love with her. Not the chick-flick-inta-lust kind of love, but the real, deep, all-consuming, give-her-all-my-tomorrows sort of love.

Which is why this hurts so damn much.

Because she was right last night when she said she didn't think things between us would work. I was a fool to think they would. It's going to hurt like a motherfucker to let her go, but the pain we'll both inflict on each other if we don't end this now will be much worse.

There will be more stalkers. More bloggers. More people who will never accept Charlie for the sweet, perfect woman she is. They'll lash out at her, try to destroy her. And I'm not sure I can protect her. Not from the whole fucking world.

So I do what I do best...I push her away.

"So about last night," I say, leaning back in my seat, not meeting her eyes.

"Yeah," she says softly. "Spencer, nothing happened with Tat—"

"I believe you."

"You do?"

"Doesn't change the fact that you went to him instead of me, that you drank to the point of—"

"I can explain."

I give a hard shake of my head. "Let's call it what it is, Charlie."

"What it is?" There's a hint of frustration in her words, and when I look over at her, I see the flicker of fire in those hazel eyes, the fight that's about to happen. "Because this is all my fault, right?"

"You're the one who went—"

"You lied to me, Spencer." Her body language matches my own, arms crossed, jaw set, gaze hard. "You told me you were going to a small gathering with your family last night, but it turns out you were at the most sought after event on campus. And I wouldn't have known any better if your ex-girlfriend hadn't insisted that I work the event."

My stomach drops. "Winslow?"

"Yeah. You've got some real class-A friends." She smiles, but it doesn't reach her eyes. "I'm starting to think it's her sole purpose to make my life hell. But in a way, I'm grateful to her because I got to see exactly who Princeton Charming is in the real world."

"Shit, Charlie, I didn't know. I'll talk to her. She won't bother you again."

She laughs, but it's a forced sound, and I see the tears gathering in her eyes. "You think I care about Winslow Harrington? I've been fighting against people like her, like Prescott, like...*you*, my entire life."

Her words do what they're meant for, slicing straight through my chest. "You think I'm like them?"

Her eyes close and she temples her fingers to her lips, not responding.

I try to put the pieces of what she says together, and I understand now why she was upset. "I didn't tell you about the benefit because I was trying to protect you."

"Protect me?" She shakes her head, disbelieving. "From what?"

"From my parents and their criticism—"

"That's complete bullshit, Spencer." She turns in the passenger seat, her eyes blazing at me. "I'm not afraid of your parents, or your uppity friends. I don't give a damn what they think about me. But maybe you do. Maybe you were too embarrassed to have me there."

I take her hand, feeling the weight of her words, knowing there's a small sliver of truth in them, even though it wasn't my intention. I hate conflict, avoid it at all cost, especially where my parents are concerned. Maybe it makes me a fucking coward.

Bringing her hand to my lips, I kiss her knuckles. God, I wish I could change the way the world works. But there will always be Winslows and Prescotts and Tatums trying to get between us.

"Any guy would be lucky to have you beside them," I tell her honestly. "I know you don't believe me, but I was trying to—"

"Protect me." She pulls her hand away. "Yeah, I

got that." Her lips turn down into a pout, and it would be cute if the circumstances weren't so dire. "But I don't need your protection, Spencer. I need your respect."

"You've got that." Even though she flinches when I reach out for her again, I cup her face in my hands and press my forehead against hers. "There's no one in this world I respect more, Charlie."

She gives a small shake of her head. "If you respected me you wouldn't have lied, you wouldn't have felt the need to hide me from your family."

"That's not what I was doing." Or was it?

Shit, maybe I am the asshole she thinks I am.

Her palms rest on my chest, that energy that's always between us sizzles and cracks, pulling, pulling, pulling, but at the same time I can feel her pushing away. No, running away.

I'm losing her.

Or maybe I've already lost her.

And I know I have to let her go, even though it's the hardest fucking thing I've ever done.

"Tonight was fun," she says, eyes filled with sadness and resolution. "But it was just a band-aid. And that photographer or stalker..." She winces with the memory of it. "It just confirms everything we already know. We hurt each other without even trying. Is it worth it? Losing ourselves..."

Except I'm not losing myself when I'm with her, I finally feel like I'm becoming the man I'm meant to be. But I don't tell her that, because she's right, around me she will get hurt.

Still...

"I don't want to say goodbye to this. To us."

Her breath is shallow and shaky, filled with emotions. "Me either, but I have to..."

I brush my lips against hers. One last kiss. "I know."

We stay locked like that for what seems like an eternity and I don't want to let her go. Not sure I'm strong enough to.

"I need you to drive me home, Spencer," she whispers, not meeting my gaze as she buckles herself in.

Fighting the tears that fill my eyes, I drive her to her dorm. When she gets out of the car, it takes everything within me to restrain myself.

Go after her, my heart screams. But even if my brain would listen, my body is frozen, and I feel a coldness settle inside me that I know I will never warm up from. Because I just let the best thing in my life walk out.

5

CHARLIE

"He still hasn't called?" Daphne asks when I glance at my phone for what is probably the hundredth time today.

"No," I mutter, feeling miserable. But I don't expect him to. Not anymore. It's been almost three weeks since Spencer and I broke up, and he hasn't called or sent even one text. I haven't even seen him on campus. It's like he's trying to avoid me at all cost.

"I know what will make you feel better," Daphne says, her eyes lighting up.

"I'm not in the mood to drink." After the night at Tatum's, I may never drink again.

"I was going to say pizza." She's already on her phone, ordering. When she puts her phone down, she grins at me. "A double pepperoni and extra cheese is on its way."

"Thanks, but I think I need to go for a walk." I put the textbook I was studying from, or at least trying to, on the table beside my bed.

I'm still not fully over the fact that she lied to me about the stoplight party, but I admit that Daphne has been extremely supportive the past few weeks.

She gives a small pout when I start putting on my coat and mitts. "But it's freezing outside."

"I won't be gone long." I force a smile wishing everything didn't feel so difficult right now. "Save a slice for me?"

"Yeah, of course," she says, but she doesn't look up from her laptop that she's now furiously typing on.

I sigh as I leave the dorm room. I've gotten pretty used to Daphne's mood swings over the past four years, but I wonder if it isn't something more. I've tried to ask her about it, but she gets defensive, and a moody Daphne is one thing, an angry one is something I try to avoid.

The snow is falling heavily when I step outside and my boots crunch with every step. I don't mind the cold. Actually, I kind of love it, especially nights like this, when there aren't many people out, and the snow covers everything in a white blanket making it look clean, new, unblemished.

I wish it would work like that on my heart.

Wish I could erase all the images of Spencer that are always in my head. The ache that never seems to go away. But I've been strong. I haven't given in to the temptation to call him, no matter how much I want to.

I've focused on my classes, and even though I've been distracted, I've managed to pull my average up another two percent. Not only should I have no problem getting into the master's program, I should be able to keep my scholarship.

Things are good. That's what I need to focus on. My mom's health has been better, and even though my dad had to sell his shop, he found work quickly. And I have a job, which thankfully wasn't sabotaged by Winslow's attempt to humiliate me. The only thing missing is...Spencer.

"It's better this way," I mutter, pulling my scarf tighter around my face. Even though I'm not sure I believe it. Sure, things are a lot less complicated without him. For one, the stalker seems to have lost interest with me now that I'm no longer Princeton Charming's Cinderella.

Then why do I miss him so much?

A door opens ahead of me and music drifts through as two people walk out of the pub. I'd been walking mindlessly and didn't realize how far I'd gone. I can't help but raise my brows when I notice that the two people are Spencer's sister, Ava, and Prescott, who look more than a little cozy with each other. After looking over his shoulder, he drags her into the shadows. Her arms wrap around his neck and his mouth is on her.

More than a little shocked, I probably stand there, mouth open watching them a little longer than I should. Okay, that's a pair I'd never have seen. Ava is sweet and lovely, and Prescott is, well...Prescott. Plus, I'm pretty sure Spencer would castrate him if he ever found out.

The two of them disappear around the corner, Ava giggling, before they notice me.

Yeah, it's an odd pair, but at least they come from the same world. They don't have an entire class system fighting against them. But still, I can't help but feel slightly protective of Ava. She's only a freshman, and while I doubt she's as innocent as I was when I started seeing Spencer, I can't imagine Prescott's intentions are honorable.

I debate calling Spencer to let him know, but

stop myself, because it's none of my business. Not anymore.

As I walk by the pub, I see Tatum and Jill sitting on stools by the window, Jill laughing at something he said. I push down the sliver of jealousy that creeps into my throat when I see them. I know they've been spending more time together lately, and it shouldn't bug me. It's not like I've been a social butterfly these past few weeks. Every time either one of them have called I've brushed them off.

I keep walking, but when I hear knuckles rapping on the window, see Tatum waving at me, I know I can't keep avoiding him. Before I even have a chance to decide what to do, he's outside wearing only a Princeton Athletic's t-shirt.

"Hey," he says, shoving his hands in his pockets, guilt still playing across his features. "I've tried to call you."

"Yeah, sorry." I glance at Jill through the window who waves at me to come inside. "I've been busy studying."

He shifts from one foot to the other, blowing on his fingers. He sounds miserable when he says, "Shit, Charlie, I'm really sorry about what happened. I know you're angry—"

"It was an accident, Tatum. I'm not upset."

"Really?" One brow raises. "Could have fooled me."

"I know. I'm sorry. I've just needed some time..."

"Yeah." He lets out a heavy breath. "Heard you and Beckett broke it off. Not going to apologize if it was about me."

"It was bound to happen eventually, right? You're the one who warned me."

He rubs the back of his neck and winces. "Didn't want to see you get hurt. That guy is a douche—"

"He's not," I say. "Whatever you think about him, he's actually a good guy."

Tatum just grunts and looks away, shoving his hands in his pockets.

Silence stretches between us.

I hate this.

"So, you and Jill?" I finally ask, wanting peace between us.

He gives a sharp laugh. "No. We're just friends."

"If you wanted to be more, I'm okay with that."

He holds my gaze and I can't read his expression. "I'll keep that in mind."

More silence.

"I, uh, should go."

"Come inside." He shivers. "It's fucking freezing out here. Let me buy you a drink."

"I don't know—"

"No whiskey, I promise." He winks.

I laugh. "Yeah, okay. Maybe just a beer."

"Good." He wraps a heavy arm over my shoulder and leads me inside, pulling out the stool he was sitting on for me before heading to the bar.

"I was starting to think you'd taken up hibernating for the winter," Jill teases, hugging me. "I've missed you. How are you doing?"

"Fine," I say with a shrug.

"Liar," she says.

I sigh. "No, really, I'm okay. What doesn't kill you makes you stronger, right?"

She groans. "God, I hate that saying."

"Yeah, me too."

We both laugh, and fall back into easy conversation. I'm not sure what made me walk in this direction, but now that I'm here, I'm glad for the company. For Jill's sharp wit, and Tatum's goofy jokes. And I feel myself relaxing for the first time in weeks. Until Jill's face scrunches in a deep frown.

"What's wrong?"

She grimaces. "Spencer's here."

My heart starts to race, but when I look over my shoulder and see who he came in with I swear it stops in my chest. There are a group of them, Georgia, Yates, a few faces that I don't know well, but it's the tall blonde who leans into Spencer as he orders a drink at the bar that is the knife in the chest.

He's with Winslow.

"Want to get out of here?" Tatum asks.

"Daphne ordered pizza. You guys could come over," I say, surprising myself. But after seeing what I've just seen, I want familiar and cozy. I want these two to keep my mind off everything else.

"Daphne?" Jill groans slightly. I know she isn't the biggest fan of my roommate.

Tatum is better at seeing the good in everyone. "She means well. And she has good taste."

"In pizza?" I ask grinning.

"No," Tatum laughs. "In picking friends."

My mouth turns to a smile at his words, and it feels good to have the air cleared with him. It's been a long three weeks.

He slings an arm over my shoulder as we walk out the door that Jill is holding open. I turn, looking over my shoulder before we step outside into the frosty air. It's Spencer's face I see, and he takes me in. It lasts a moment, a flash, but I see it. The hurt in his eyes.

Once again I'm tucked against Tatum.

The same way Winslow is pressing herself against Spencer.

I suppose old habits die hard.

6

SPENCER

THE SMELL of the gardenias overpowers the table, but Mom has a thing about floral bouquets. She spends her afternoons creating arrangements in her greenhouse and places them everywhere she can. Today they are front and center at family brunch.

My father sneezes for the third time. "Christ, Suzanne, get those things off the table."

Roz, the housekeeper who has been with us since we were children, scoops up the arrangement and carries it away without a word, she is nearing seventy and has learned a few things over the decades. Mainly, don't raise an eyebrow during my parents' spats - but if things become too demanding ask for a raise. They always oblige because losing Roz would be a blow for every last one of us.

"It's not my fault you didn't take your allergy medication, Geoffrey," Mom hisses as she sets a napkin across her lap.

"I suppose it's also my fault that you waste your days—"

Ava cuts them off. "I seriously did not take a train from Princeton just so I could listen to you bicker for twenty-four hours."

When our parents aren't traipsing across the country campaigning, or schmoozing with the other one percent, Ava and I try to make the trek to our parents' D.C. home once a month, another weekend they come to Princeton, and then there are two glorious weekends a month where we can avoid them altogether.

I'm leaving as soon as the quiche is finished.

"When you have a husband you'll understand how tolerable I actually am," my mother says placidly as she reaches for her mimosa.

Ava merely twists her lips, and I know something is on the edge of her tongue. "I actually went out with someone last week."

"Who?" I bark, a little too loudly. Ever since things ended with Charlie, I have been a fucking wreck. I think about her incessantly, dream about her daily, get off to the memory of her perfect body every time I touch my goddamn cock.

It's gotten me a bit on edge.

Ava notices. "God, Spence. You're the one who needs a..." She bites her tongue on whatever crude thing she was about to say, and mutters, "Girlfriend."

Mom perks up at that. "You and that little waitress are no longer an 'item?'" She actually uses air quotes.

I look at Ava, silently thanking her for keeping my personal business to herself. It would have been easy to bring it up to my mother considering she's like a hyena on the prowl for gossip regarding me. Because of it, I drop the subject of whoever she's been seeing as a way to say thanks.

"Calling Charlotte Hayes a little waitress is inexcusable," I say without concern for anyone's feelings but Charlie's. I loved her. *Love her*. "I won't have this conversation with you unless you can be—"

"Oh for God's sake, Spencer," my father mumbles, waving his hand in the air. "Stop being so damn politically correct."

I scoff. "Aren't you a political strategist?"

"Yes, but that doesn't mean half of what I strategize isn't bullshit."

This isn't new territory, I've been through these murky waters plenty of times with my father. It's the reason I let Ethan take over the ship's wheel years ago. Prescott may think it's because I'm scared of failure - but that's only in part. The other part of me reels at my father's stance in most political issues.

I want to take hold of my ship now, and I don't want my father's help. However, that conversation is best saved for another day.

For now, I just want to get through this meal and get back home to Princeton before dark.

"You boys love to rile up your father," Mom says, but as she lifts her mimosa to her mouth, her face falters. As she sips, we all consider her slip up.

You boys.

There is no you boys anymore.

Ethan is gone.

Ava reaches over and squeezes Mom's hand and my shoulders soften, knowing we've all had a hell of a few years. The last thing we need is to have a fall-out over fucking gardenias or ex-girlfriends.

Ex.

God, it's so damn final. It kills me to think that Charlie and I are truly over.

Dad's eyes meet mine. No matter how pretentious he might be, old money written on his wristwatch and cufflinks - I know he hates to see his wife and daughter in pain. He still has a good heart.

At least I choose to believe he does, because if he doesn't, what does it say about me?

"Let's have a toast," he says, raising his glass.

"To what?" Mom asks, blinking rapidly. As if images of Ethan are flashing through her mind's eye.

"To family," my father says, his distinct voice sending a ripple through the room. A current we don't often express. Love.

I lift my glass to meet his, Ava's eyes glistening with tears. We may be a fucked up family, with our priorities all out of order, but sometimes - on rare occasions - we let our guards fall and truth is revealed.

We may be Becketts, but we're also human, after all.

ON THE TRAIN back to Princeton, Ava is quiet, reading a science textbook until she dozes off. I pull out my phone, needing to touch base with the guys Prescott had put me in touch with after the incident ages ago with the rock through Charlie's dorm room window.

"Malcom there?" I ask.

"It's me. What's up, Spencer?"

"Just wanting to check in on everything. Is there an update on the surveillance? I usually receive a report at the week's end, but haven't gotten anything yet."

"Fuck, sorry, yeah, I've got it ready, just wanted to add last night's data."

Most of the reports consist of basic information. Who she was seen with coming and going from her dorm. If there was any suspicious activity at night. Nothing has been flagged as potentially dangerous. Thank fucking god.

But even though he was able to retrieve the video of Charlie and me in the library, it had been a burner phone, nothing to tie it to any individual.

"Was there something out of the ordinary?" I ask, rubbing my temple.

"No, she was just with that guy. The football player?"

The words make my skin bristle. Trying to sound nonchalant, I ask, "What were they doing that needs to be added to the report?"

"Uh, gimme a sec, I'll pull it up and send the

footage to you. My guy was on it and I haven't even looked at the feed."

I grunt, wondering exactly what I'm paying him ten grand a month for if he doesn't even bother to make sure Charlie is safe around the clock.

"After you look at it, let me know if you want us to check on anything else, honestly, because there haven't been any red flags since we started."

"Understood," I say, ending the call. A moment later my phone chimes and I pull open the grainy video. A streetlight shines down on Tatum and Charlie as they run across the quad toward her dorm building. She reaches to the ground and grabs a handful of snow before pelting Tatum with it. He returns the blow with a snowball of his own, before running toward her and tossing her over his shoulder.

Her face is bright, even through the black and white recording. I can practically hear her laughter, feel her joy.

My heart goes cold. That love I felt as my family and I sat around the dining room table, leaves my body. She is happy. Without me.

I close the video and open the text thread. I quickly type a message to Malcom. *Thanks for the help, but we can close down the recon. Charlie isn't in need of my help anymore.*

It's the truth - and it slays me to type it. But I press send anyway. Charlie never asks for full-time surveillance and am no longer the man in her life.

Ava stirs, sitting up and running a hand through her hair. "You okay?" she asks, her voice still sleepy.

"I'm fine." Which is a big fucking lie.

She pushes out her bottom lip. "You miss her?"

I lean my head back against the chair and breathe out, "Yeah."

She reaches in her bag and hands me a bag of chocolate covered pretzels. "Here. These make everything better."

A second later my phone chimes again.

"Who is it?" Ava asks.

"Prescott." I turn it to silent. I knew he'd be calling, asking about why I just ended things with his buddy Malcolm, but I don't want to get into it. Not tonight.

"You should take it," Ava insists. "He's your best friend."

"Oldest friend," I clarify. "There's a massive difference."

She shrugs and looks out the train window. "He isn't so bad."

I smirk. "Tell that to the two juniors he had at his place last night."

Her gaze jerks back to me. "He had people over at his place last night?"

I roll my eyes. "Yeah, that fucker knows how to brag about his threesomes, I'll give him that. He's trying to remind me there are more women in the world, more fun to be had."

"I see," Ava says curtly. "Then maybe you were right. Maybe Prescott isn't worth talking too." She excuses herself to use the restroom.

I shake my head at her moodiness. I'm not blind, I've seen the way she's fawned over Prescott since she was a kid. But the douchebag is smart enough to keep his hands and other body parts to himself.

With Ava gone, I text Prescott instead of calling. Truth is, I need his honest opinion in my life. I miss it - his blunt edge, his no-nonsense desire to make something of himself. I need that drive. And I know pushing him away isn't going to help me get where I want to. My father may be an asshole, but he has friends that have always had his back. Prescott is my wingman as much as I'm his.

I'm done holding grudges. It's time I fucking moved on.

God knows Charlie has.

Me: I ended things with Malcom because I'm trying to move on.

Prescott: Does this mean Princeton Charming is officially back on the market?

Me: IDK. Was thinking politics, not pussy.

Prescott: You know, you can have both.

Me: No thx. But I want to talk about this summer.

I see three dots, then silence.

Several minutes pass and I wonder where Ava went off to. Eventually my phone chimes again.

Prescott: Sorry. Girl problems.

Me: You break someone's heart?

Prescott: More like talking a girl off the ledge.

I smirk. Same old guy.

Me: Maybe we can help one another after all. Politically.

Prescott: So I'm no longer banned to the bad boy's corner?

Me: No guarantees.

Prescott: Will you be such a ball buster when we get to D.C.?

Me: Depends on if we go together or not. You in?

Prescott: You know it motherfucker.

When we pull up to the station, a car is waiting for Ava.

"Who's that?" I ask.

"Just an Uber. I'm good from here." She pulls me into a quick hug before heading off to the town car. "Love you, Spence. And hey, maybe give Prescott a break. I think he means well."

"I think he does too."

I see a shadow of someone in the backseat, and her smile broadens as she opens the door. I watch her go, hoping she is better at picking boyfriends than I am at being one.

Charlie deserves to be happy, and so does Ava.

7

CHARLIE

I NEVER CHECK my phone while I'm in class. I know plenty of students do, but I am here with one aim: to graduate with honors. And I know that won't happen if I'm texting - or like the girl sitting next to me in Advanced Environmental Science - sexting. I've accidentally glanced her way one too many times when she's been sending a full frontal shot. Not my thing. At all.

So when we're in the middle of a lecture and my phone starts ringing, I instinctually freeze. That can't be me causing my professor to pause and then groan while looking for the culprit.

When he sees it's me, his gaze softens. Maybe it's because I've been consistently contributing to class discussions, but I'm guessing it's because as my hands wrap around my phone, I start to panic. Tears in my eyes, shaking. Fear.

The only reason I could get a call while my phone is on silent is if my parents try to call me three times in a row.

It could only be one thing: an emergency.

"Dad?" I ask as my father's muffled sobs break through the line. I'm standing with my bag on my shoulder, pushing my way past the sexter, eyes brimming with tears as my Professor nods understandingly. In the hall I ask - no, I implore, "What happened?"

"Charlie, it's your mom. She..." His voice shakes and my hands do too. "She's gone. She...passed away sweetheart."

No.

No.

No.

I can't take a breath and I feel like I'm drowning. But when air finally hits my lungs, it comes back out in a guttural cry that shakes through me. My sobs echo through the long and prestigious corridor of the lecture hall. The ceilings are cavernous, high and hollow and my heart is undone. He says words I try to absorb. But it's impossible to take anything in when the pain is so ragged, so raw - so absolutely unexpected.

Complications from her MS. Heart attack. Unexpected. Emergency room. Tried to save her. Gone.

I try to listen, to focus but all I see is a world without my mother and it's a world I don't want to live in. A doctor calls to him and he has to go. "I love you, Charlie," he manages, his heartache palpable.

"I love you, Daddy," I say, but the words are muffled by my cries.

Blurry-eyed and hysterical, I wind my way out of the hall, needing a plane. Now. Needing to fly to my father so I can wrap my arms around him, be his strong-hold, be his shield. He can't be alone right now. How will he live without her?

She was his rock, his world. His everything. Now he's alone in a sterile hospital, making decisions he wasn't prepared to make.

I reach for the handrail as I walk outside, stumbling as I crash into the bright sunlight. It shouldn't be sunny today. It should be a dense fog, hanging low, it should be slashing rain and smoldering thunder. It should be dark. So dark.

How can you miss someone so deeply when they've only been gone a matter of minutes?

"Charlie?" Spencer's voice reaches me from somewhere I can't see. The tears are swallowing me up whole. "Charlie, woah, there, hey, I got you. I got you now," he is saying, his arms wrapping around me as I fall against his chest.

I breathe him in. Sandalwood and leather and promises we couldn't keep. I miss him.

"Charlie, what happened?" he asks, his arms tight around me, his hand smoothing my hair. I burrow closer to his chest, his thick wool sweater catching my tears and my body goes limp against him. Terrified of a world without my mother.

I can't talk and he must sense that. He picks me up off the ground and he whispers that everything will be alright and maybe for him, it will. He has his family and money and a life all mapped out and mine just got pulled out from under me. What is the point of any of this if you don't have the ones you love with you at the end of the day?

Time escapes me when I'm in his arms and then as if by magic we are in my dorm. He's found my keys in my bag and the room is empty, just like my heart and he sets me on the bed and gets me a glass of water, but I can't drink. Can't breathe. Can't think.

"She's gone." My shoulders heave and my stomach turns, and I need my dad.

"Who's gone?" he asks, kneeling before me on the floor. Perfect Spencer Beckett. With his thick hair and bright eyes and heart-melting smile. He cups my face and our eyes lock and in that moment, he holds my sorrow.

It's just long enough for me to collect myself.

Not to put myself together, no - just enough for me to take a deep breath. To exhale with the words I prayed I'd never have to say, "My mother just died."

He doesn't ask a single question. What is there to know? In my eyes, he saw it all plain enough. The life I had before is not the same as the life I have now. My mother is gone, and I wasn't with her when she took her last breath. I wrack my mind for what we spoke about on our last conversation and all I remember is a text thread about the afghan she was knitting.

How can that be the last thing we talked about?

I cry against Spencer because he is here, but also because he knows me in ways no one else on earth does. When we were together, our bodies entwined, he gave me the greatest nights of my life. And now we are sharing my lowest low.

When my shoulders stop shaking, when I finally have the strength to reach for the glass of water, after I gulp it down all at once, he asks, "Did she suffer?"

"It was a heart attack," I say. "Which, after everything, all the surgeries, treatments...all of it...it seems like the cruelest way to go."

Spencer nods. "I'm so sorry, Charlie. It's not fair."

"How could her heart fail her? She had the purest heart of anyone I've ever known."

"I don't know," he says and the fact that he doesn't try to have all the answers brings on a fresh flood of tears. I'm so glad he's here with me right now. I don't want to imagine being in this room right now, alone.

"You need to get home."

"I know. I need to get a ticket." My head starts spinning with things I need to do and I don't want to do any of them. All I want is to give my dad the biggest hug in the world and never, ever let go.

"Shhh, shh, Charlie, breathe," he says, and he pulls out his phone. "I'll get you home tonight, I promise."

I swallow, grateful that he's here, believing that his swift and steady decisions will get me back to

Michigan faster than anyone else on the planet could.

"Will you come too?" I ask as he begins to speak with a travel agent.

He pauses his phone call, steps toward me, and squeezes my hand. "I'll be with you as long as you need me."

8

SPENCER

It's a Thursday afternoon and thankfully the flights aren't full. I book us first class tickets for a flight leaving in two and a half hours. It's tight, but we will make it. We don't plan farther than one foot in front of the other. I just need to get Charlie home.

When Charlie is in the bathroom washing her face so we can go, I make a few necessary calls. She packs quickly and I call Prescott, he lives a block away from my townhouse.

"It's an emergency," I tell him. "I need a bag packed. Black suit. I'll be there in twenty minutes."

"Fuck, who died."

I run a hand over my jaw. "Charlie's mother."

Prescott knows enough to discreetly end the call

and promises to have my bag ready for when we swing by.

Then I get us a car and help Charlie into her coat. She's shaking, in shock, and my heart fucking breaks for her. It's wrong, every last thing about it. Heather was young, generous, a fighter. And now she's gone.

My chest tightens as I try to imagine Charlie's father, Daniel, right now. A salt of the earth man, with tears falling down his cheeks. All too fucking much to bear. This kind of pain can crack a person in two. And it might be years before they start piecing themselves together.

I know it all too well.

We get to the airport quickly, and when we get to the gate, Charlie's shoulders fall all over again as she sees who's here, waiting for her.

She crumbles as Tatum wraps her in his arms.

"How did you get here?" she asks. "How did you know?"

He kisses her forehead, his eyes glassy, same as mine. "Spencer called. Got me a ticket. Made sure I was here. For you. God, Charlie." He wraps her in his arms again, and this time I have to look away.

I bought him a ticket, knowing he is Charlie's

best friend. Maybe more than that for all I fucking know.

And I'm glad he's here, she needs him here. Wants him here.

But God, it fucking slays me.

When it's time to board the plane, I'm grateful that the tickets are printed with our seating arrangement. I don't want to decide where Charlie sits. With whom. Not at a time like this.

"We can board now," I say, doing my best to hide the jealousy that tightens my throat. She wanted me with her, that says something, right? And even if it's just as friends, I can accept that, just to be with her, to support her. It's better than nothing.

Tatum's hand never leaves Charlie's back as we board the plane and I see him frown when we get to our seats. It's probably the first time he's flown first class, but I know that's not what bothers him, it's the fact that Charlie is seated next to me.

I return his hard look when he takes his seat, because in all fairness I could have put more distance between them than a fucking aisle. And the only reason he's even here at all is for Charlie.

"Thank you for doing this, Spencer." Charlie's

fingers twine with my own and she rests her head on my shoulder.

I can feel her strength slipping. I know what comes next, the emotional and physical crash as the adrenaline wears off. The next few days will be a vicious rollercoaster of emotions.

"You should try to get some sleep," I say, pressing my lips against the top of her head.

"I don't think I can." She yawns as she says it, and I can already feel her body sinking into the leather chair beside me, her head becoming heavier on my shoulder.

"Just try."

It's not long after we're in the air that I know she's out, her hand still in mine. Tatum glances over at us, not hiding his disapproval, but smart enough to keep his mouth shut.

Without disturbing Charlie, I pull out my phone and scroll through the missed calls and texts. Nothing urgent, but I respond to Ava, who somehow already knows about Charlie's mom.

Brat: Prescott told me. Is there anything I can do?

There's a niggling at the back of my head questioning why Prescott is talking to my sister, but I push it aside. He wouldn't touch her, not unless he wanted to lose his balls.

Me: Yeah, I need you to go to the Montgomery Fundraiser in my place tomorrow night.

Brat: Sure. No problem. Give Charlie a big hug for me.

Me: I will.

Ellipses dance on the screen before another message from her pops up.

Brat: You really do love her, don't you?

I sigh, wondering if it's that obvious to everyone. I shove my phone back in my pocket and signal the flight attendants to bring Charlie a blanket and me a drink.

Charlie sleeps until the captain announces that we're starting to descend. She's groggy when she wakes up, and I feel rather than see when reality hits. Fresh pain rolls off her and I hear her small gasp like she's trying to take in air, but can't.

It'll be days, even weeks before that goes away. Even now, more than two years after Ethan's accident, there are moments that I forget he's gone. Moments like my mom had at breakfast a couple weeks ago.

"Just breathe," I say against her ear, feeling her anxiety, her panic. "I've got you."

Her eyes close, and she takes small steadying breaths. "It doesn't...doesn't feel real..."

"I know." I squeeze her hand and hold her gaze, the anguish in those hazel eyes undoing me. Part of me thought staying away would protect her, but I realize now that there's always going to be pain in this life.

"I keep going through our last conversation together. I can't remember..." She shakes her head. "I can't remember if I told her I loved her."

"She knew you did, even if you didn't say it."

Charlie nods, her eyes glassing over with memories and emotions. I let silence wrap around us, knowing there are no words that can take away the pain she's going through.

"You doing okay?" Tatum asks, reaching his hand across the aisle toward her.

She lets out a shaky breath and gives a small nod. I try not to flinch when she takes his hand.

She's not yours anymore, my brain reminds me.

But fuck, the thought of her being his guts me.

There aren't many words exchanged as we collect our luggage and meet the car I ordered. We sit sandwiched in the back seat, Charlie in the middle, as we drive toward her hometown.

There are multiple cars parked along the curb in front of the small one-story house as we approach, and I can see shadows moving inside.

"My uncles are here," Charlie says as I help her out and gather her bags. "The house is going to be busy."

"Do you want me to come in?" I ask, wanting to be here for her anyway I can.

Tatum has come around the car and places an arm over her shoulder. "Just let us know what you want, what you need."

"I think..." A tear rolls over her cheek and she brushes it away with the back of her hand. "I think I just need to go in alone." She looks at me. "If that's okay."

"Like Tatum said, whatever you need. I've got us rooms at the Kensington. We'll just be a phone call away."

"Thank you." She wraps her arms around my neck and hugs me.

I hold her, probably longer than necessary, long enough to earn me a scowl from Tatum, before helping her bring her luggage to the front door.

The tiny house is crowded, and Charlie is swept up in a whirlwind of hugs and sobs before the front door closes on me. Damn, I want to be in there. To be her strength. And it guts me that I'm not. Maybe if I hadn't been a pussy all those weeks ago, thinking I was protecting her by walking away, I would be.

I walk back to the car where Tatum is pacing.

"We should stay." There's a tick in his jaw, and he looks like a bull ready to plow through the closed door. "She'll need...us," he says the last word like it's got a bitter taste.

"What she needs is her family." I open the door and get in. "She would have asked us to stay if she wanted us in there."

His palm slaps down on the roof in frustration before he moves around to the other side, slamming the door when he gets in and looking about as miserable as I feel.

I still haven't forgiven the fucker for hitting her, even though I know the shot was meant for me. But I have no doubt that the bastard loves her. And even though I hate him for it, I also can't fault him. Charlie is...everything.

"Hate leaving her," he mutters as the driver pulls away.

Me too, but I know it's what she needs.

I pull out my cell and scroll through my messages. "She needs time to grieve, alone."

"Okay, Dr. Phil." He rolls his eyes at me.

I glance over at him and narrow my eyes. "You've never lost anyone you love, have you?"

He grunts. "And you have?"

"Yeah," I say simply, holding his gaze. "And it fucking sucks."

"Shit." He rubs the back of his neck. "Yeah, I heard something about your brother. Sorry, man."

I shrug and glance out the window. The last thing I want to get into right now is a deep conversation about life and death with Tatum fucking Madden.

After I check us into the hotel, I hand him his keycard.

"You didn't have to do this?" he says as we ride the elevator up to our floor.

"Yeah, I know," I mutter. "Didn't do it for you."

"You're not the complete douchebag I thought. But that doesn't mean you're good enough for her."

I grunt. "And you are?"

He shifts the duffle bag on his shoulder as we get off on the third floor. "I want to be. And I don't need you coming in and messing everything up again."

My chest constricts. "So you two are together, then?"

Outside our rooms, which are right beside each other, Tatum holds my gaze, and I can see he's thinking about how to answer.

Finally he says, "No. Not yet."

The asshole inside of me stirs. "Good." I bite back what I really want to say, and use my keycard to open my door.

"You'll just hurt her again," Tatum says, obviously not ready to let the subject go, and I see the need to fight in his eyes.

I get it. It would feel good - no, it would feel fucking terrific right now to let out some of my tension on him. But the last thing Charlie needs is for both of us to show up at her mother's funeral with black eyes and bloody lips.

"Enjoy your room," I mutter. "Try and keep the porn charges to a minimum."

"I love her." His declaration echoes down the hall, and straight through my chest.

I guess we're doing this. Here. Now. I toss my bags in the entranceway of my room and turn to him.

Maybe if I wasn't a selfish prick, I'd submit, knowing in all fairness he probably is the better man. I've done some digging into his past. Other than a speeding ticket he got senior year of high school, the guy is as wholesome as Wally Cleaver.

But is that really what Charlie needs? What she wants?

Maybe. Or maybe what my Cinderella really needs is her prince.

"I love her," Tatum repeats, jaw bouncing, hands flexing into fists. He looks like he just declared war rather than love, but I guess that's what this is.

"Yeah, I know," I finally say, gaze locked on his, and admit, "But so do I."

9

CHARLIE

"Here, Dad, let me help," I say when I see my father struggling with his tie, his hands trembling as he tries to undo his failed attempt at a Half Windsor.

"I don't know what I'd do without you Charlie," he says as I manage to knot it correctly. My own hands shake, but I try to conceal that from my dad. He's been on the edge of collapsing over the past forty-eight hours, and the last thing I need is another parent in the hospital.

My body has been going through the motions, talking to the funeral director, ordering the flowers, writing her obituary, and I've forced myself to close off the emotional parts of my heart and just be the support Dad needs.

But now it's the day of the service and it's all hitting me so hard.

"I can stay as long as you need, Dad," I tell him, meaning it.

"You have to get back to school, you're so close to being done."

I smooth down the collar of his shirt, unable to meet his eyes. A tear slides down my cheek. "And what will you do? Without the shop and without Mom?"

"Freddy offered me a job."

"In Chicago?" I frown. My three uncles live there, it's where Dad grew up. But the idea of him no longer being in Michigan, of this no longer being the place I return for holidays and breaks, it cuts deep.

But I know it's probably for the best. At least he wouldn't be alone. With my mom sick, he got good at taking care of the house by himself, but I don't like to think of him all by himself in this house. And yet, the thought of him moving even further away, him selling my childhood home, well…it sucks too.

My dad places a hand on my shoulder, and he lets out a long uneven breath. "Let's talk later, after…"

"Okay." I wipe my eyes. Freddy's wife, my aunt

Lydia, is a little bossy, but she's healthy, and I know she'd make sure Dad was okay. "I just...I need someone to look after you if I'm not here."

He gives a forced smile. "I'm still young, I have some fight in me left."

"I know, Dad. I just hate the idea of you being alone."

His eyes well up with tears and he presses his hand to his heart. "Your mother will always, always be right here, Charlie. Always."

"I know." I swallow the small sob that builds in my throat.

From the breast pocket of his jacket, he pulls out a necklace. Her necklace. A gold chain with an aquamarine pendant. My birthstone. My dad bought it for her when I was born, and she wore it every day of her life. "I want you to have this."

"You're sure?"

He nods and when I turn he brushes my hair aside, clasping the necklace around my neck.

I move to the mirror, Dad behind me, my fingers running over the cool stone that she always had hanging so close to her heart.

"You look just like her," he says.

"I hope I *am* like her, too. She was…"

"Everything."

I nod. "Yeah, she was."

Dad and I leave the house in our black coats and black gloves, climbing into a town car that Spencer ordered. It's so much more than my father could have afforded on his own, and I'm grateful for the gesture.

Spencer has been so steady the last few days. So strong. When I'd first met him, I thought his charm was surface level, but I've seen him differently as he has so graciously supported me throughout this tragedy. I didn't expect it - I know he has a politician's heart, but I've realized he also has compassion that goes beyond volunteering at a homeless shelter. He cares about people, deeply.

He cares about me.

Without any expectations. And I wish he was by my side right now. I need his strength. I've tried so hard these past couple of days to be strong for my dad, and I'm not sure how much longer I can keep up the act.

The funeral hall is full when we arrive, and Dad puts his arm around my shoulder as we walk down the aisle toward the front pew.

There are so many people. So many emotions. And the framed picture of my mom in front of the casket makes my throat squeeze so tight I can barely breathe.

Suddenly I doubt my ability to read the memorial I've written for her. I press a hand to the slip of paper in my pocket, wondering how I will summon the courage to speak to so many people.

We pass piano students she taught over the years before she got sick, some of the nurses who took care of her throughout her many hospital stays, and other faces that I don't know, but from their tears obviously touched in some way by my mom.

I see Tatum and Spencer in one of the pews near the back, and I manage a small smile when our eyes meet. But when I reach the front and come face to face with my mom's casket, I feel my strength leave me. And yet it's nothing compared to the deep sob that breaks from my dad's chest.

It's all too much.

My dad's brothers are beside him when he drops to his knees in front of the casket, and I'm glad because I know I don't have the strength to support him. I'm not sure I have enough strength to stay standing myself. But then a hand is under my elbow, a familiar scent wrapping around me, and Spencer is leading me to the reserved pew.

"I ca-can't do this," I whisper, choking on the words.

"You can. You're strong, Charlie. And I'm right here."

I look up at him, blue eyes full of the strength I need, filled with understanding, compassion. When it's my turn to go up front and say a few words, my eyes meet Spencer's, and I feel him silently urging to be brave. Tatum, beside him, gives me a smile that reminds me that I'm not alone in any of this.

My aunt thought it wasn't necessary for me to give a few words today at the service, but I insisted. I am my mother's only child, her daughter. Her legacy depends on me.

I want to make her proud.

Sucking in a shaky breath, I twist the paper in my hands realizing they aren't the words I want to say after all. Mom was music and a clear voice, and these words feel too heavy.

"My earliest memory is of my mother singing to me," I share with the room. "She always carried a tune, always in the right key. We didn't always have a lot, but we always, always had music. She taught me to love it before she taught me to read. It's a gift I am forever grateful for."

I look over the crowd, finding my father. He's

smiling now, remembering, and that fills my heart with peace, allowing me the courage to continue, "I'm not a singer, and I can't play the piano for the life of me. When she tried to teach me, my fingers fought the keys, whereas hers always sailed over them. But she never told me she was disappointed. Never told me I wasn't enough." I wipe the tears spilling down my cheeks, the memories washing over me. "She accepted me for who I was. Even if I had a chip on my shoulder, she saw it as a strength, never a weakness. Mom was soft, with a gentle grace I've always admired. And the world was better with her in it. I love you, Mom, forever."

I step away, hugging my father, he kisses my cheeks, and we sit, side-by-side as one of her friends plays "Wind Beneath My Wings" on the piano. I'm grateful she volunteered to play, but my mother would never have chosen this song. It makes me wish I had spent more time trying to learn myself. When I look up at Dad though, his shoulders shake, the love he has for my mother palpable, and I realize this song wasn't for me. It was for him.

The entire service seems to last hours, even though I know it's only scheduled for forty-five minutes. By the end of it, I'm emotionally and physically drained. Whoever decided that it was a good idea for grieving family members to stand in line and greet a hundred-plus strangers must have had a sadistic heart. Because by the time I've shaken the last hand, heard the last *I'm so sorry for your loss*, I just want to curl up in a ball and sleep for a week, or maybe a year. However long it will take to make my heart feel whole again.

"Drink this." Spencer is beside me, at the end of a hallway, placing a cup in my hand.

When I take a sip, the whiskey burns my throat and I relish it. We decided against a graveside burial, and most of the family and friends are still congregated in a room at the funeral parlor for coffee and cookies. The idea of walking in there, sitting at a sterile table and hearing people reminisce about my mother makes my heart ache. The whiskey, on the other hand, numbs me in the best possible way.

"You were so brave," he tells me.

I sink against the wall, and when a woman passes us, I look to the floor, too exhausted to meet anyone else's gaze. "My uncles are taking my dad home."

"Do you want to go with them?" He leans close, blue eyes searching and willing to do anything I ask.

God, I love the man. And right now I need him more than I ever have.

I shake my head, taking another sip. "They're Irish, they'll be drinking this stuff all night," I say, lifting the cup. "I don't want to be there."

Spencer's suit coat is snug against his broad shoulders, his hair falling across his brow. He steps closer to me, tucking a loose strand of hair behind my ear. "I didn't know you were Irish."

I pinch my fingers together. "This much. But according to my uncles, we're full-blooded."

Tatum is at the other end of the hall and I see him looking around, coffee and cookie in hand. He's looking for me. I'm glad he's here, but it's not Tatum that I need.

I blink away the tears that keep pooling in my eyes.

"I'm glad he has his brothers tonight," Spencer says. I know he's remembering his own brother. Remembering so much.

I look up at him, both lost and found. "I'm glad I have you."

10

SPENCER

I KNOW Charlie needs to get out of here.

Now.

She's exhausted and needs to rest, without having to offer anyone an explanation, offer anyone - even her father - support. She needs space to grieve.

I'll give it to her.

Give her everything.

I get her in her coat, stand with her as she says her goodbyes to her dad. Promising to have her back tomorrow. And then she's in my rental car, and we're leaving the funeral home, and I pull up a playlist, the one I made for today. For her. For whatever might come next.

Little darling, it's been a long cold lonely winter.

Charlie sighs as "Here Comes the Sun" begins to play, and she unrolls her window even though it's February and it's fucking freezing out and there is frost on the ground and ice on the window.

I realize she unrolls the window because a crack of light breaks through the clouds.

"The snow is melting," she murmurs. "Spring is coming."

I look over at her, our hands held tight as I drive through the town that holds so many of her stories, the good and the bad, and I am in awe - of her beauty and her strength and her pure heart.

And I wonder how the fuck I ever let her go. How the hell I let her walk away. Because I know that even though she is way too good for me, if I could do it all over again, I'd find a way to be the man she needs.

I will find a way to be the man she needs, my heart promises, not giving my head a chance to argue.

The sun is so bright as it streaks across the horizon and I want to chase it - that stretch of light. I want to chase it with her.

I realize then, that unshed tears burn my eyes. Not just tears for all this loss, but for the life I want. The life I want with her. That's what this girl does to me. Makes me hope, and wish, and dream. I saw how much her parents loved each other. They may not have had a lot, but they had each other, and that was enough.

I get it.

Because Charlie is my enough.

We get to the Kensington and I wrap my arm around her shoulders as we pass through the lobby, silently leading her to my room. I notice Tatum's door across from mine. I know she never told him goodbye this afternoon. For a fleeting moment I wonder if I should remind her to call him, text, but then we are in my room and she is in my arms and her mouth is on my lips and I will give her anything. Everything she wants.

Still, I ask, "Are you sure?"

"I need you inside me," she whimpers. "I need to feel something besides this ache."

"I'll give you anything, Charlie. Anything you need. But—"

"Then take me away from this moment." Her eyes are pleading, and she whispers, "Please."

So I do. I give her exactly what she wants, what she needs.

I undress her slowly, so slowly my cock begs to be released. So slowly she is weeping with want. So slowly that there is nothing between us but unsatiated desire. Her dress. Her stockings. Her panties. Her bra. She is naked and bare before me, my clothes are shed and my hands run over her skin. I hold so much raw beauty in my fingers that it fucking slays me.

She is a treasure, a princess, a miracle.

"I need you to fuck me," she breathes, the words so uncharacteristic, so ragged and rough, that my mouth crashes against hers.

I want her to know she can be soft with me too. That this can be about more than sex. That it can be about forever.

But right now she is blinded with pain and I can do her the honor of taking her away from it for one night.

My fingers run over her wet pussy, leading her to bed. God, how I've missed her body, her sweet lips, her round tits, and her skin so fucking soft I could bruise it.

But I won't. I'll be gentle with her until she begs me to be rough.

Her body opens up to me like it hasn't been a month since we've been together. Like it hasn't been dozens of sleepless nights when I jacked off to the memory of her creamy slit, of my tongue running over her as her knees buckled and her back arched.

Her knees part and I run my hand over her wet pussy, my fingers pressing against her throbbing clit and then move deeper inside her. She needs this. Me.

And so do I.

She wraps her hand around my cock, and I groan - unable to restrain myself. Not wanting to. She can have as much of me as she wants. God, how I wish she wanted it all.

"You're so hard," she moans as I kiss her neck, leaning over her. I send a trail of kisses down her sternum, sucking her tight nipples, kissing her until I know I'll leave marks. Wanting to claim her any way I can.

She screams my name as I begin to fill her tight pussy, my cock moving deeper as she pants for breath. I kiss her to silence her but also to inhale her. I want her all, I'll take what I can. It's only one night but goddammit how I wish it were forever.

She cries as I fuck her the way she demands. Tears streak her cheek as I make her pussy drip, and I release deep inside her, my hot cum filling her up the way we both need.

Completely.

Sitting up, I cross my legs, pulling her onto my lap, and she wraps her legs around me. Her arms wind around my neck, and I wrap mine around her - pulling one another close - our bodies become one as she sinks against me. Our eyes lock as we move together in a tight and desperate rhythm. Every inch of our skin connects and it's intimate in a way we've never been before.

She comes against me, her body slick with sweat and hot with desire and her eyes search mine and I don't know what she is hoping to find.

I want to tell her I love her because I do - but she's here with me to disappear, not be brought back to the present.

So instead of words, I make love to her. Offering her everything I can give, knowing there may be nothing in return.

But deep down I know I already have more than I deserve.

I have this. *This.*

11

CHARLIE

Warmth and heaviness surround me as I stretch, blinking when a stream of morning sunlight fills the room, and I realize that it's Spencer's body that's draped over mine.

I fell asleep in his arms last night, and every time I woke up, a sob in my throat, he was there to comfort me with words and kisses and more. I know I just complicated things by asking him to have sex with me. We're broken up and one night doesn't change that.

But it was what I needed.

To lose myself in him.

To forget.

And for a few moments, I did.

I wish I could stay here, in his arms. It doesn't

take the pain away completely, but it makes it somewhat bearable. And yet I know there are so many things I still have to do. My dad still needs me, and my uncles and aunts will be expecting me back at the house this afternoon.

When I roll over, Spencer's face is only inches from mine, his eyes closed, long lashes casting shadows over his cheeks, his dirty blond hair disheveled, and dark scruff coating his chiseled jaw.

My heart speeds up, filled with so much love for the man. God, I wish things could be different. But nothing has changed. He's still my Princeton Charming.

No, I remind myself. He's not mine anymore. As much as I wish he was.

I place my palm on his face and his eyes flutter open.

"Hey, beautiful," he murmurs sleepily, pulling me tighter against his chest. Eyes locked, we share a silent moment. Just him and me. No grief. No world outside this room. Just us.

But then there's a loud knock at the door and he's sighing, rolling out of bed, grabbing his pants and putting them on.

After I grab Spencer's shirt and pull it on, I

check my phone which has been on mute since we left the funeral parlor.

There are a dozen texts from Tatum, and I realize that I never said goodbye to him before we left. I'm mid-texting him back when I hear his voice behind me.

"She's not texting me back. I'm worried that—" Tatum freezes when our eyes meet.

Spencer leans against the open door, still shirtless, hair tousled, and it's obvious what we were doing all night.

"I just got your texts now," I say, walking toward them.

Tatum's gaze is hard and his jaw bounces as his gaze skim down my body, taking in the oversized button-down and bare legs, then back up to my face. And I know he's hurt.

What can I say to him? That it's not what it seems? Because it is. And he has no claim over me, despite the anger and jealousy that tugs at his expression.

"I was just texting you back." I give him a small smile, but he doesn't return it.

Nostrils flaring, Tatum swallows hard and his gaze turns to Spencer. "I was wrong, you really are a douchebag. Taking advantage of her when she just lost her mom."

"Careful Madden," Spencer warns, moving slightly so that he's in between Tatum and me.

"I asked him to bring me here," I say, moving between them, which you think I would have learned my lesson from.

The right side of Tatum's face twitches and he looks down at me. I can see all the things he wants to say, the harsh words, the lecture, but he just shakes his head.

"I'm heading back to school this afternoon. I just wanted to let you know."

I glance back at Spencer and give him a look, telling him to give us a moment. He does, walking into the bathroom and shutting the door. A few seconds later I hear the shower turn on.

Wrapping my arms around myself, I lean where Spencer was a moment before. "Thank you for coming."

He rubs the back of his neck and glances up at the ceiling before saying, "I'm trying here, Charlotte. Really fucking hard. I don't know what you want from me."

"I want you to be my friend."

"I don't know if I can do that." He scrubs his

hands over his face, looking completely miserable. "I'll always be here for you, but I don't know if I can...can't watch you with *him* again."

"I'm not with Spencer. It was just one night. But if I was, it's not fair to ask me not to see him."

"Not fair?" He chuckles, but the sound is hollow. His fist presses against his forehead and he closes his eyes. "You're grieving, I get that. You needed someone to lean on. Just wish...wish it was me."

I hug him, and his arms wrap around me. Tatum is one of my best friends. I don't want to lose him.

"I love you, Tatum," I mutter against his chest.

"Yeah," he says, cupping my jaw so I look at him. "I know." He gives me a sad smile. "But you love him more."

I pull my bottom lip between my teeth and look up at him. "It's just different."

He sighs and drops his hands, then takes a step back. "I'll see you back at school, Charlotte. Call me if you need anything, and..." He starts to walk away, then says over his shoulder. "Tell the douchebag thanks for the plane ticket."

I shut the door and press my forehead against it,

wondering why everything has to be so complicated.

"You okay?" Spencer asks. A towel is wrapped around his waist and his skin is still damp.

"No," I admit, falling into his arms when he opens them to me. "But I will be."

THE HOUSE FEELS EMPTY, it's no longer home without Mom here. I've spent the morning sorting through Mom's record collection, debating what to put in a storage unit until after I finish school and have my own place.

"You need to go back to school." My father is in the kitchen, packing Mom's china and silverware into boxes for storage. "I'm going to stay with Freddy and Lydia. I'll be fine."

I can see Spencer through the large front window, shoveling snow with my uncles, his face red, and he laughs at something they say. It warms my heart, him here with me, but I know things are going to change when we go back to school.

I'm starting to realize that everything changes. Nothing is constant. Not life, or relationships, or homes.

"But the house." I sit on the couch, knees pressed against my chest, feeling like I'm twelve years old again with absolutely no control over what happens. I'm glad my dad has my uncle and aunt to help him through his grief, but my heart aches that he's already contacted a real estate agent and plans to have the house listed next week.

"As much as I want to keep this place..." He chokes on the words, back hunched over. He has moments of quiet strength, and then grief consumes him. I feel it too. "I wish I could keep the place for you, for your mom's memory..."

I stand and wrap my arms around him. "I know."

And I do. But the small profit he'd make on the house will pay off some of the debt he acquired over the years. It's not an easy decision for him, and me acting like a spoiled child isn't helping.

"It's okay. I understand."

He pats my back, then wipes the tears from his eyes, turning back to packing. "Is Tatum coming over today?"

"No, he went back to school." I'm still not happy with the way we left things.

"I know I'm not your mom..." My dad rubs his

neck, looking awkward. "But if you need to talk...about...boys..."

"Thanks," I say, glancing back out the window at Spencer. But there are some things that daughters and dads don't talk about. Some things a girl needs her mom for. I suck in a shaky breath as it hits me fresh all the things I'll never be able to share with her.

I'm glad my dad doesn't press me about Spencer and my relationship, because honestly, I'm not even sure where we go after what happened last night. He's still here, shoveling my driveway, making stupid jokes with my uncles...that has to mean something, right?

"What is it, Charlie?" Dad asks, setting down the dishes in his hand. "What aren't you saying?"

I bite my bottom lip. "How did you know Mom was the one? I mean, I know you met in high school, but...how did you know you loved her?"

Dad lifts his eyebrows, looking out the window at Spencer. "Corny as it sounds, she was my match. My equal. With her, life made sense."

"I know, but like, what was it? Specifically?"

Dad sits down next to me on the couch. "It was a hundred things and it was nothing. It was the fact that she was there, always. My constant. My best friend." Dad chokes on his words. "I'm guessing you're asking about Spencer, that you're falling in love with him?"

"I don't know if the way I'm feeling is the kind of love that is lasting or if it's something else."

Is it grief that has my heart spun up so tight? Is it lust? How do you know if the way you feel is enough? Last time it didn't work between us. What has really changed now?

"Your mom was the person I thought of when I went to bed, when I woke up each day. Do you feel that way?"

He looks out the window, Spencer is clapping my uncle Freddy on the back, laughing. The winter air making his features more crisp, more clear. He takes my breath away. Is that enough?

"What will you do now, Dad?" I ask, looking up at the man who shaped me in so many ways.

"Charlie, I have twenty-five years of your mother's love in my heart. I'm going to be okay." He squeezes my hand. "And you have all that love she gave you in your heart. It means you'll be okay too."

"I love you, Daddy."

He kisses my forehead. "Maybe it's time that chip on your shoulder melted."

I frown. "Why?"

"Because you can't fall in love, completely, if your edges are too sharp."

"You think I should become a teddy bear like you?" I smile.

"No, I think you should be you. Don't pretend to be someone else to fit in another person's world."

I smile, not used to hearing my dad talk like this. "When did you become such an expert at love?"

He wipes his eyes, and even in the midst of so much sorrow, in this moment, all I see is joy. "Your mother was a good teacher."

I swallow, a sense of peace blossoming inside me for the first time in days. When I leave for Princeton, I know my dad is going to be okay.

And I'll be okay too.

12

SPENCER

"You are in so much trouble," my sister says as she walks through the door of my place, cheeks flushed pink, her blonde hair still perfectly coiffed despite the wind that whips and whistles outside.

Like our mom, she has that same way about her that always looks put together. But as she takes off her jacket, making herself at home, she has an impish grin, and I can tell whatever trouble I'm in she's going to enjoy seeing me squirm.

"What are you talking about?" I shut my laptop and stretch out on the couch, legs crossed on the coffee table in front of me. "And how did you get a key?"

She rolls her eyes and goes to the liquor cabinet, pouring herself a scotch. "I took your spare off your keychain during orientation week." Her nose scrunches when she takes a deep swallow of the gold liquid.

"A little early for that, don't you think?"

"You'll want one too when I tell you who's going to be here in..." She checks her phone. "Um, twenty minutes."

My back teeth clench, and even though I have an idea who my impromptu guest is, I ask, "Who?"

"Mom. Apparently she heard about your little"—Ava makes air quotes while holding the crystal glass in one hand and her phone in the other—"donation."

"Shit." I check my own phone, but there aren't any messages from her, which is worse than if there was, because now I'm about to receive her full wrath in person.

I knew she'd find out eventually. The million dollar donation to the MS Society that I made in Heather Hayes' name came from the Beckett family fund, which my mom oversees. I just didn't expect her to come all the way to Jersey to confront me about it.

"So how is Charlie?" Ava asks, sitting across from me.

"As good as can be expected," I say, even

though I haven't spoken with her since we've been back.

I'm here if she needs me, but I also don't want to push her.

"So are you two, like back together?"

"No." I drag my hands over my face, then back through my hair, that familiar feeling of frustration and agitation building.

"But you totally hooked up again, right?" She smirks at me knowingly.

I give her a hard look. "Not discussing my sex life with my little sister."

She laughs, but then her expression turns serious. "I actually need to talk to you about something."

"If it's about *your* sex life, I really don't want to hear it," I tease. But when she frowns at me, I realize that's exactly what it's about. I sit up, taking my legs off the coffee table and leaning forward. "If someone hurt you, give me their name and I'll—"

"It's not like that." She fidgets with her glass before pouring herself another three fingers of the thirty-year-old malt.

I stand and walk toward her, knowing I'm not going to like whatever she's about to tell me.

"What's it like then?" I ask, towering over her, my big brother instincts on high alert.

"I just want you to promise me you won't get mad."

I take the scotch from her and drain it. "Can't promise that until I know what you've got yourself mixed up in."

She sighs. "I'm not mixed up in anything. I'm just...dating someone."

"Who?" I narrow my eyes at her, because even though I know my little sister is far from innocent, I can see her trepidation in telling me.

"You have to promise—"

"Just tell me who I need to beat the shit out of."

"See." She shakes her head at me. "That's why I haven't said anything."

"Fine," I say, sighing. "I promise. Just tell me who it is."

She chews on the inside of her lip, blue eyes filled with anxiety, which only makes that protective side of me even more on edge.

"It can't be that bad—"

"It's Prescott."

I grunt. "Yeah, right." I pour myself another drink. "Seriously, who is it?"

"I am serious. We've been...together for a few weeks now. I really like—"

"Don't play games." Anger builds in my chest, and I pray to fucking God she's making this shit up.

"I'm not. He wanted to wait to tell you, but—"

"Jesus, Christ, Ava," I spit out, slamming the crystal glass on the counter.

"You promised you wouldn't get mad."

"If he touched you—"

"Spence, we're dating."

I tug at my hair, needing something to do with my hands, because right now I'm ready to wrap them around the bastard's neck. Of all the chicks on campus and the sleaze puts his slimy hands on my sister. But I'm not sure who I'm more upset with, him or her.

"I thought you were smarter than that. You know who the bastard is. All the girls he's screwed. What do you think is going to happen? Shit, Ava, he was just bragging last week about having the Reagan twins—"

"It was a lie. He made it up."

"Just tell me you haven't fucked him."

"So what if I have. It's my choice."

"Goddamnit, Ava." I cup the back of my head with both hands and look down at her like she's lost her mind, which I'm pretty sure she has. "He's a player, a user, whatever the fuck Prescott has said to you, you can't believe a single word."

"That's funny coming from Princeton Charming." Her face is red with frustration and she crosses her arms glaring up at me defiantly. "How many people said the same thing to Charlie? Prescott loves me—"

I laugh, hard. "You're bullshitting me, right? Prescott loves one person, himself. He's using you, Ava. I'm not sure what his game is...to get back at me, or for our family's name..."

"You've always seen the worst in him."

"Because there isn't anything good in him."

"Nice way to talk about your best friend." Unshed tears make her eyes glisten. "I thought you'd understand, after everything with Charlie. People can change—"

There's a knock at the door before it opens and my mother walks through. The energy in the room is already heightened, the tension palpable, so when she starts into her lecture before she's even said hello, I snap.

"I don't need your shit right now, Mom."

Her delicate hands flutter to her chest, and her

mouth opens in shock. "How dare you talk to me like that."

"Sorry." I take in a few steadying breaths.

Ava is still on the verge of tears and despite how pissed off I am, I pull her toward me and hug her, hard.

"I need you to be okay with it, please," she says against my chest.

"What is going on with you two?" my mother demands.

I sigh and pull back, looking down at my sister. "I can't be okay with it. You don't know him like I do."

"You're wrong." My chest constricts at the pure, undulated devotion I see in her eyes. And I wonder how long she's been in love with him, and why the hell I hadn't noticed it before.

I could argue circles around her, tell her things about the man that would make a sailor blush. There are a lot of things I'd call Prescott Addington, and good isn't one of them. But I'll deal with him later.

And after this, we're done. Some things are just unforgivable.

"If the two of you are done with the theatrics, I didn't come here to be ignored."

I squeeze Ava's shoulder before turning to my mother. "I'm guessing you're here to talk about the donation. But before you lay into me, that money is meant for charity—"

"To be given in the Beckett name."

"So that's what you're upset about? Not that I donated the money, but that you won't get recognition for it? Classic."

"Oh for goodness sake, I've raised you better than this," Mother scoffs.

"You know what, after the week I've had, the people I've met, I have no patience for my family."

Ava takes in a sharp breath. My mother's eyes go stone cold. "You had plenty of patience for your family when you made the donation."

I run a hand over my jaw. She has me there. I do value the money my family has, it gives us the ability to do good in this messed up world. Unfortunately it isn't so simple as that - Mom coming here is case in point.

"This is exactly why I want to make my way in the world on my own, everything you offer has strings."

"Spencer, you may have spent a few days in middle America in a fantasy land with that gold digger—"

"Don't, Mom, don't do this," I say as evenly as possible. "If you cross this line, I don't think we can come back from it."

"Is that a threat?" my mother asks, her manicured hand on the strap of her gold chained Chanel bag. She hasn't even been here long enough to take off her coat.

"It's a promise."

Ava's eyes are wide, and she reaches for our mother's hand. "Why don't we let Spencer cool down, Mom? He's had an emotional few days and—"

I don't dignify her with a response. I want them gone, now. I open the front door, the February frost greeting me. Silence follows them as they leave my house, as they walk away.

Slamming the door shut, I punch the wall, anger swelling up in me.

But I won't be a victim. I've let fear dictate way too much of my life already.

It's time I figure out my own life like a motherfucking man.

13

CHARLIE

My phone buzzes on the table beside my bed, but I just groan and pull the comforter over my head. It's Saturday, the one day I don't have to get out of bed, and I don't plan on moving. Since being back, it's like a heaviness has settled over me. A numbness. I still have moments of grief, that makes my throat tighten and tears pool, but for the most part, I just feel...empty.

I haven't heard from Spencer. He told me to call him when I was ready, but even though I want him here, need him beside me, I just can't muster the energy to dial his number.

I left Michigan in a good place. I helped get Dad settled into his brother's house, and our family home is on the market. Of course, I'm heartbroken over Mom, but the reason I've been a zombie is because I'm exhausted. The last few weeks zapped me of all my energy. There is nothing in reserve to give anyone right now, let alone Spencer Beckett.

The only thing I've been able to do is go to class, pick up a couple shifts at the restaurant, and come back to my room and sleep. Essays are due soon, and I have a test next week that I'm not prepared for, but I just can't seem to care.

The door opens and shuts, and the lights flicker on, followed by Daphne saying, "Get up. You need to eat."

I groan. "I'm not hungry." I haven't had an appetite, and I know I've lost weight. But everything tastes like sandpaper.

The comforter is pulled off me, and Daphne stands at the edge of the bed with two bags from Chipotle. "You're going to eat, and then you're going to get up and shower, because honestly, this room is starting to smell like a guy's locker room."

I force myself to sit up, knowing I should be grateful for her persistence, but just wanting to go back to sleep.

"Thanks," I mumble, taking the bag from her, my stomach rumbling when I open it.

She sits on her own bed across from me, and

pulls out a taco, then takes a bite. I do the same, and I actually feel a little better when I do.

"I know you don't feel like getting out of bed, that it's easier to just sleep away the sadness, but you have to force yourself to keep living." Daphne gives me a sympathetic look. "I know what you're feeling..." She puts her taco down and hesitates before saying, "I mean I haven't lost my mom, but I know what it's like to feel like you're...drowning."

"I'm okay."

She gives a sad smile. "You barely get out of bed. I'm pretty sure you haven't showered in three days, and your hair..." She smirks at me. "Let's just say the whole dreadlock thing went out of style years ago."

I touch my matted hair and grimace. "Is it that bad?"

"It's pretty bad." She sighs. "Maybe you should go talk to someone. There are counselors who deal with grief—"

"I'll be fine."

"I used to say that too. Until I wasn't." She rubs her wrist where an old, white scar starts and runs halfway up her forearm. When I'd asked about it in the past, she'd said it was from a car accident, but now I'm wondering if it's something more.

"What happened?" I asked, grateful to think about anything other than my own grief.

Her brows are pulled down, lips thin and she looks lost in a painful memory before she says. "I saw something...something terrible. And it changed me." She meets my gaze, and it's the first time that I feel like she's ever truly let her walls down, like I can see deep into her soul...and what's there is pain.

I can see she wants to open up, to share, but still, something holds her back.

"I suffered from depression." She shrugs, but I know it's not something easy for her to admit. "It's like...like you're swallowed by this giant black blob and the harder you struggle to get out of it, the tighter its grip becomes."

"Yeah, that's exactly what it feels like."

"Can I tell you something?"

I nod. "Of course."

"I've always been kind of jealous of you. How strong you are. You don't take any bullshit from anyone."

"I don't feel very strong right now." I glance out the window. It's snowing hard, and like everything it reminds me of Spencer. I felt so much stronger when he was by my side. But I don't want to be that girl, the one who needs a guy to make her feel complete.

"You know what you need?" Daphne is grinning at me, mischief in her eyes.

"No, but I'm guessing it has something to do with alcohol and sex," I tease.

"Damn right," she says. "You need a night out."

"I really don't feel like it."

"That's the point. You won't feel like doing anything but sleep for a long time. You have to force yourself to get out."

"No parties."

"Okay, then how about we catch a movie, then maybe stop and have a couple of drinks?"

It's the last thing I want to do, but I know she's right.

I nod. "All right."

She claps her hand. "Perfect. But before we do anything, you really need to shower."

I chuckle. "Yeah, that's probably a good plan." I reach for the Chipotle bag, my stomach growling for the first time in days. "But first, tacos."

Daphne laughs, pulling out the take-out food she ordered us. "There is always time for tacos."

"That was seriously the worst movie I've ever seen," I say as we leave the theatre and head toward the Triumph Brewing Company.

Daphne laughs. "It was pretty bad, but I wasn't really paying attention to the plot. Anything with Henry Cavill in it and I'm mush. He totally would have made the perfect Christian Grey."

"I was totally pulling for Charlie Hunnam."

She feigns shock and starts into a lecture why he would never have been able to pull off the role. "Sure he's hot, but he's not Christian Grey material. First, he's blond—"

"I like blonds," I say.

She rolls her eyes. "Yeah, we all know that already."

"What's that supposed to mean?"

"Princeton Charming," she says as we reach the Triumph and a guy opens the door for us.

"I thought it was your rule not to bring up his name."

She grunts as we take a seat at the bar. "I'm just glad you finally smartened up and kicked his pretentious butt to the curb."

"I'm not really sure it was me who broke it off with him...we just...I don't know."

Daphne orders us two Hurricanes, then turns to

me. "Well, whatever happened, you're better off without him."

"Why don't you like him?" I ask. She's never really given me a good reason.

There's a flicker of something in her eyes, something I can't read, before her face stretches into what I know is a fake a smile. "Who said I didn't like him? I just didn't want to see you get hurt."

"You sure that's all? I know he has a reputation. Did something happen between you—"

Daphne looks at me sharply. "I would never do anything with a Beckett."

"Okay," I say softly, resting a hand on her arm. "I didn't mean anything by it." Still, I feel a little bruised. If she is so adamantly against hooking up with Spencer, what does that say about me? About me falling for him?

Falling in love with him.

When the waitress returns I order a molten chocolate cake. Sugar makes even the most tense conversations better. And something has shifted between Daphne and me since we sat down at this restaurant. I wish I'd never mentioned Spencer. Though, now that I think of it, it was Daphne that brought him up.

"Look," she says, obviously recognizing the

tension that is settling between us. "I want you to be happy. After everything you've just gone through, the last thing you need is a boyfriend who doesn't respect you."

I frown. "Spencer respects me. It's not that. It's just...complicated." I exhale, thinking aloud, "And I haven't even called him all week, now he's probably hurt that I haven't reached out."

Daphne lifts her eyebrows. "And Tatum, he's out of the picture?"

I fill her in on his awkward departure and she grimaces. "That's pretty bad, Charlotte. Seeing you in Spencer's bed the day after the funeral. Yikes."

"I know, right?" I moan. "I didn't mean to break his heart. What he needs is a rebound."

As the waitress delivers the cake, I notice a group of guys being seated at the table next to us.

"Decan's here," Daphne says under her breath. "Do you want to go?"

I look over at the table, Decan's eyes are on mine for a split second, but then he's pulled out his phone, moving on. Good.

I pick up a fork, then hand one to Daphne. "I'm staying here and eating this ooey, gooey piece of perfection. I'm honestly a little tired of making sure every guy on campus is emotionally stable. I'm focusing on me tonight."

Daphne smiles, her bubbly laugh helping me relax. She lifts her cocktail. "To girl power."

"To badass princesses," I add, laughing.

Daphne grins. "Exactly. You don't need Prince Charming. You're already a queen."

14

SPENCER

After I kicked my sister and mother out of my house, I spent the week avoiding my father's phone calls. But I know I can't put it off anymore.

"Would you like to tell me why your mother has been crying for days?" he asks roughly.

"Not particularly."

"I don't want to get in her business, but you must understand her position. The Beckett name carries weight and when we make donations—"

I cut him off knowing I'll pay for it later. "You know what, Dad? What I really wonder is when you stopped caring about the rest of the world? Or were you always so self-centered?"

The line goes silent. I told my mother not to

cross any lines with me, but I realize I just crossed a line with my dad.

"Spencer, we don't always have the luxury of doing exactly what we want, when we want it. But if you want financial support from this family, you need to rein yourself in. Now."

"Understood," I say, realizing for the first time, that it's not his money I want. It's his respect.

And why? His politics don't line up with mine, his values are skewed, and his priorities have always been self-serving.

We hang up, not agreeing to a single thing, but feeling the line in the sand. It's been drawn. Now I can decide if I want to cross it, and when.

Wanting to clear my head, I pull on my winter coat, wrap a wool scarf around my neck, tug a beanie on my head. Then I turn my phone off and leave it on the kitchen counter. Part of me thinks Winslow might try calling today. Last year we spent this day together and she gets all kinds of sentimental no matter how often I remind her we are through.

I lock the front door and step out into the cold. The fresh air does me good, and I forget about my thesis paper for a moment, forget about the argument with my family - the fight I know I'll be having with Prescott soon enough. Instead I walk without a destination in mind, the only twinge of regret I have is leaving my phone because now I can't pop in earbuds and listen to music as I walk.

But, as I turn the corner, the record store comes into view, and it feels serendipitous. Without hesitation, I step inside the small shop, the warmth of the store washing over me. Hardwood floors and aisles of records. The Temptations "My Girl" plays from speakers and there is no way you can't smile when you hear the iconic love song.

I know I don't fit in with this store's typical clientele. Punk and grunge and hipster are the words one might use to describe the shoppers thumbing through vinyl records, but no one even turns to look up at me, no one pays attention to my Burberry coat and gloves. They are too busy enjoying themselves.

It relaxes me, the lack of pretension. The easygoing shop owner with full sleeves and a dozen piercings, who asks if I need any help. The little girl who has on headphones, sitting on a beanbag in the corner, her t-shirt reading ABCD with a lightning bolt in the center, her pink tulle skirt the perfect juxtaposition.

I'm not looking for anything in particular -

besides an escape, maybe, when I look up and see Charlie staring at me from across the aisle.

"Spencer," she says softly. She looks tired. Worn. I remember the weeks and months after losing Ethan, I hung on by a thread. She looks like she could unravel.

"Charlie," I say, stepping closer. "How are you?" The question feels so formal, so stiff. What I really want is to wrap my arms around her and kiss her cheeks and tell her how much I miss her. Every hour of every day.

She pulls off the emerald green beanie that was slouching on her head, her hair a tousled mess. Her eyes look down, she's in a pair of silver Uggs, thick red tights, a bright orange peacoat, a yellow corduroy skirt.

"I know," she says with a laugh. "I look like a troll threw up all over me. I was hoping that wearing bright colors would cheer me up. But I don't know if that's the way it works."

"At least you're trying."

She smiles easily, eyebrows raised. "I suppose. Though, it's mostly because Daphne was threatening me with a Hallmark movie marathon if I didn't get dressed and leave the dorm."

Worry knits itself across my face, and she must notice.

"It's okay. It's not that I'm depressed, I just don't have a lot of extra energy to put into...life."

I don't like the idea of Charlie going to a dark place, alone. I want to help pull her out of it.

"I think you look cute. You look like a Funfetti cake."

She smiles. "What does Spencer Beckett know about cake mix from a box?"

I fake offense. "Hey, my parents may be the one percent, but I'm still American. Everyone loves Funfetti cake."

She laughs, and the sound fills my heart, feeds my soul. It's been a long time since I've seen Charlie happy and it's the most beautiful thing I've ever fucking seen.

"God, I miss you," I say, without editing myself. Unable to. I need her.

She runs a hand through her messy hair, not meeting my eyes. "Sorry I didn't call."

"Don't apologize. This is your life, you can do with it what you want."

She nods. "I know. But still, I should have."

"Why didn't you?"

She fingers the beanie in her hand. "It's been

hard being back here and I kind of retreated. I leaned into myself instead of reaching out."

"There's a time and place for everything," I say. "Don't be hard on yourself."

"I've missed you too, Spence."

"Yeah?" I ask, swallowing hard. Not wanting to get my hopes up.

She nods. "Yeah."

I take a chance. "Are you up for getting a coffee? There's a little shop across the street." Her brows narrow and I add, "As friends."

The corner of her mouth tugs up. "Your treat?"

"Always."

15

CHARLIE

When I left the dorm this afternoon, I didn't expect to run into Spencer. Maybe if I had, I would have pulled a comb through my hair or looked for clothing that matched. But ironically, I don't feel self-conscious in front of him even though I look a thousand kinds of looney.

I feel seen.

We find a corner table and begin peeling off winter layers and then Spencer goes to the counter for our drinks. He returns with two white mugs towering with whipped cream and red heart sprinkles.

"Those are cute," I say.

He lifts his mug and lightly clinks it against mine. "Happy Valentine's Day."

My eyes go wide. "It's Valentine's Day?"

Spencer chuckles. "Yeah, you missed the memo? The record store was playing only classic love songs."

I groan. "No wonder Daphne was in such a sour mood. She was whining about not having a date the moment she walked in the door with a pint of ice cream and plans to Netflix the heck out of the night."

Spencer takes a drink of mocha, when he sets down his mug, there is whipped cream on his nose. I swipe it away, with a sudden urge to do so much more. To lean closer. Close enough to kiss.

I blink, knowing that is ancient history. We are ancient history. I don't even want to know what he thinks about the way I begged him to have sex with me after my mother's funeral. He must think I'm a mess at best, desperate at worst.

"So um, how have you been?" I ask, wanting to get the attention off the fact I am sitting here with my ex-boyfriend on the most romantic day of the year.

He tenses. "Things have been...fine."

"We've been through enough together, don't you think? You don't need to pretend. What's up?"

"It feels trivial in light of what you've been going through, is all."

I twist my lips. "So is it a school issue, a future issue, a family thing, or friend drama?"

He laughs. "Those are the four categories?"

I nod.

"Well school is fine, grad school hours are pretty nice. But the other boxes would all get checked."

"Yikes," I say, taking another sip of the chocolatey coffee, grateful to have something to talk about besides my own grief. "What happened? Did someone try and dethrone Princeton Charming?"

"My sister is dating Prescott, if you can believe it."

I shake my head, remembering seeing them together a few weeks ago and not believing it then. It's hard to imagine sweet Ava with the calculating Prescott. "I can't see it."

"Me either." Spencer runs a hand through his hair, he looks so handsome when he does, his muscles strain and my core tightens. God, I've missed him.

"So I'm assuming Prescott and you are fighting about that?"

Spencer sighs. "Actually, we've been doing a

pretty stellar job of avoiding one another. It was Ava who told me."

"And your parents, what do they think of the new relationship?" An unexpected knot tightens in my stomach. The idea of the Becketts accepting a man like Prescott but not a woman like me hurts more than I'd like to admit.

"Truth is, I haven't really gotten into it with them. We aren't exactly on speaking terms at the moment."

"How come?"

He winces and looks away. "It's nothing."

"Obviously it's something. What happened."

"I made a small donation, that's all."

"A donation to what?"

He sighs and leans back in his chair. "I guess you'll probably find out anyway. After the funeral, I used the Beckett trust to make a donation in your mom's name to the MS Society."

Emotions swell inside me. I've never liked it when he used his money to buy things, but this is different, this is...Spencer.

"And your parents are upset?"

"I'm pretty sure they'd find any reason to be pissed at me lately. But I wasn't exactly easy on them either."

I place my hand over his. "I know your family isn't the most accepting, but they're still the only one you've got."

"Yeah, I know you're right." His fingers twine with mine and his gaze goes distant as he looks at where our flesh meets.

Energy sizzles and snaps between us, that constant pull.

"I should be heading back," I say, knowing where this will end if I don't walk away. Me begging him for one more night in his arms.

"I'll walk you." He stands and offers me his hand.

I take it and we leave the coffee shop.

"So no big date tonight for the infamous Princeton Charming?" I ask, teasing, but also curious about if he's seeing anyone else. It shouldn't matter, but it does. And I'm not really sure I want to know.

I feel him tense.

"Sorry," I mutter. "It's none of my business."

He stops and places his hands on my shoulder, his jaw bouncing, blue eyes hard. "I'm not seeing anyone, Charlie, if that's what you're asking. Haven't since..." He glances away and a flash of pain tightens his features. When he looks back at me, his gaze has softened. "Since we broke up."

"Oh." What else can I say? I lean into him, knowing I'm falling down a slippery slope. But I can't remember one good reason right now why we're not together.

I fist my fingers into his jacket, snow falling around us, and his hands go to my face, cupping my jaw, gazes locked.

God, I love him. My chest aches with it.

"Spencer—"

"I know." He gives me a sad smile and rests his forehead against mine. "Just friends."

Except I want so much more. I want him.

I wrap my arms around his neck and pull his mouth to mine. He kisses me back. Soft. Gentle. His lips brush against mine hesitantly.

"Friends don't kiss, Charlie," he says roughly against my mouth, his fingers curling in my hair at the nape of my neck, and I can feel him holding back. Feel all the pent up emotions that we've both shoved down.

"Maybe we can make an exception?"

His breathing is ragged. "You're killing me, Hayes."

"Sorry." I start to pull away. Maybe I misread the situation. "I shouldn't have—"

He kisses me hard then. His tongue swiping past my lips, his mouth taking, consuming. It's a lot, and still not enough.

I'm lost in the kiss, my body melting into him, my fingers desperate to touch him and hating the material that separates us.

Women's laughter pulls me out of the moment. A group of girls that I recognize from my dorm are walking by, and one of them has their phone out, no doubt recording us. But it's the guy she's with that gives me pause.

Decan has his arm slung over the blonde's shoulder, his expression violent, lips curling in a sneer.

"We should go," I say, stepping out of Spencer's arms.

"Yeah, sure," he says, frowning. I'm not sure if he's even aware of the people watching us. Or of Decan. But I don't want any trouble. I take his hand and we start to walk in the opposite direction of the group.

When we're outside my dorm, I stand on one of the steps so that I'm eye to eye with him. "Thanks for walking me back."

"What are we doing, Charlie?"

"I don't know."

He exhales a rough breath. "I fucking hate this."

"Me too."

Silence wraps around us. Not being with him is torture. But nothing has changed. He's still Princeton Charming. And no matter how many times I've fantasized about being with him, I can't see a future, a life where we can make it work. His family and friends will never fully accept me, and I don't want to be part of a world that constantly snubs its nose at me just because I wasn't born into the top one percent.

But right now, with him standing in front of me, all those things don't seem to matter.

"Go away with me this weekend," he says, moving closer.

I lick my lips, wanting his on mine again. "Where?"

"The mountains. We can go skiing."

I laugh. "I don't ski."

"Yet," he says, his eyes sparkling with hope. "I'm a good teacher."

"Okay, Princeton Charming. You can teach me

to ski," I say, thinking of all the other things Spencer Beckett has already taught me - most of which took place in a bedroom, not the ski slopes.

I stand on my tiptoes, kissing him again. Quick this time, with the promise of more.

16

SPENCER

"You sure we can't just stay in the lodge?" Charlie asks, biting her bottom lip, her eyes wandering longingly toward the fireplace flanked by oversized leather armchairs. An older woman is sitting with a Kindle and a hot toddy and Charlie is practically drooling.

I shake my head. "No, I'm getting you on the mountain. From the sound of it, you've hardly left your dorm in weeks. The fresh air will be good for you."

She sighs but doesn't disagree. "Hot chocolate first, though?" she asks, pointing to a coffee stand in the lodge.

I chuckle. "We just had coffee."

"That was like, an hour ago. I need a sugar rush

before I strap myself into the skis."

"I think you just have a sweet tooth."

She smiles, scrunching up her nose as she drags me to the coffee stand. "Well, that too."

We stand in line for her drink, and she laces her fingers with mine. I don't know what we are exactly, if we are dating - but being here at this lodge, away for the weekend, makes me believe that anything is possible.

"Why are you smiling?" she asks, standing up on her tiptoes. I wrap an arm around her. God, she looks so cute in this winter hat and scarf.

I look into her hazel eyes, flecked with hope, same as mine. "I'm just happy you came, Charlie."

"Me too." She kisses me quickly on the nose, laughing, and then turns and places her order. Then we step aside to wait for her drink. "When I told Daphne I was coming she didn't believe me. And Tatum has strong opinions about this trip."

I'm sure he does.

Still, I frown, not sure where this is headed. She squeezes my hand. "But there is something here. Between us. Something I wouldn't expect my friends to understand."

"Hot chocolate for Charlotte," the barista calls.

Charlie reaches for it, pulling off the lid and

taking a sip of the whipped cream laden drink. We walk away from the coffee stand, into a corner where we can be alone.

"And the thing is, Spencer, seeing you on Valentine's' Day felt … serendipitous."

"I didn't know you believed in fate."

She bites the corner of her lip, lifting her eyebrows. "I believe in us."

I picked her up early this morning, and our car ride to the mountain was comfortable. We listened to music and drank our to-go cups of coffee, she told me about the term paper she is getting a head start on and I told her how I spent last weekend at the homeless shelter in Manhattan.

But the words she is saying now - they're different than friends playing catch-up.

Now that we're here, and she isn't backing away from this. Us. What we could be. She's leaning in, same as me.

"I'm really glad we're here, alone, so we can figure out what we want," I tell her, choosing my words carefully. Not wanting to jump the gun. Confess everything. Things I have no business saying but want to share all the same.

That being in Michigan with her changed me.

That not having her in my life is torture.

That she makes me want to be the best fucking version of myself.

Our bags are in the room where we'll be staying tonight before we head back to campus tomorrow. We just got here and I'm already dreading the idea of leaving.

She smiles. "Yeah, you can find out if you really want to spend time with a girl who has two left feet."

She offers me her hot chocolate and I take a drink. "I've never thought of you as a klutz. And if I remember correctly, you have some impressive dance moves."

Laughing, she takes her cocoa back. "True. Maybe it's all a defense mechanism. It's a little intimidating being up here with you. You grew up skiing, I grew up making snowmen."

"Then let's get out on the slopes and see what you're made of."

She shakes her head, but she's smiling. "I don't think you realize what you're getting yourself into. Tatum tried taking me snowboarding once and it was a disaster."

I frown, thinking of Tatum being on a mountain with her. The idea of the two of them up here makes my skin crawl.

"You are so jealous," she laughs.

"It's hard imagining you with someone else, is all."

She takes my hand in hers. "Well, you're the one with me now."

I pull her into a kiss, loving the way she fits so well in my arm, and even though our weekend away has only begun, I have high hopes.

The way her lips melt against mine tell me I have good reason to dream.

"See," she whispers as we pull apart. "We could just go up to the hotel room and do more of that...no need to wrangle with ski poles when you have a pole—"

I cut her off, teasing. "I see what you're after here. You're looking for an out. But I promise this is going to be fun. Besides, you went to all that work getting the gear you're wearing, might as well put it to good use."

She laughs. "True." She runs a hand over the white snow parka her friend Jill let her borrow. She has on a cute white hat and white snow pants that are way to big for her. "I wish Jill and I were closer to the same size, I feel like a giant marshmallow."

"I think it's cute. You're a snow bunny." I pinch her nose, aching to pinch so much more.

"You'll be calling me the abominable snowman the moment I step off that lift," she laughs.

I push open the heavy wood door, the majestic mountain cutting a gorgeous view for us, the bright sun blazing down and the sky blue. It's the perfect day.

"Is that Winslow?" Charlie asks, pointing over at the ski rack, frowning.

"Fuck me."

Charlie laughs. "Anxious, much."

I chuckle, appreciating that Charlie doesn't get all wound up over seeing my ex. God knows I'm not quite as cool with Tatum. "I didn't know she would be here."

"It's okay, she doesn't even see us."

"Yet," I mutter under my breath as we pause for a moment, waiting for Winslow to walk away before heading toward our skis to clip ourselves in.

When we're finally all geared up, I begin explaining how to maneuver.

"Just bend your knees and waist slightly," I tell her. "Yep, just like that."

She adjusts her body and listens for the next directive. "And keep your arms out wide."

Like the focused student she is, she asks, "How wide exactly?"

"As if you're about to hug someone."

She smirks. "I wouldn't mind peeling off these layers and hugging you. Naked."

I belly laugh. "God, I didn't realize the snow made you so horny, Ms. Hayes."

She purses her lips. "I'm trying to distract so we can make a new game plan."

I relax, setting a hand on her arm. "Look, we don't have to do this, I just thought it would be a fun way to get your mind—"

"No, it's fine. I'm just giving you a hard time."

I look down at my groin. "Hard is right." Then smacking her butt, I add, "No more jokes about stripping out of our clothes until we get down the mountain, okay?"

"Bossy," she deadpans. "I like it."

I shake my head, laughing, as I explain that she needs to feel her weight evenly on the balls of her feet and heels. Charlie may talk down about her ability, but she is relatively coordinated as she uses the poles to help push her forward after she has a grasp of how to stand.

"You're doing great, babe."

"Well," she says with a good-natured grin. "If it takes us until lunch to get down the mountain, I'll sign up for a lesson. Deal?"

"Wow, already underestimating my abilities to teach you."

Minutes later we're at the front of the line for the ski lift and climbing aboard. Two lines merge as one, and before we know it, Winslow is joining us.

"A little snug for three?" Charlie asks as the attendant keeps the line moving, sending us up.

"I called for you back there," Winnie says. "You must not have heard me."

"I was pretty occupied." I look at Charlie and grin. "Who are you here with anyway?"

She rolls her eyes. "Connery begged me. His family planned a ski trip, and his twin brother is here with his fiancée. So, our Connery needed a fake girlfriend."

I snort. "That's the nicest thing I've ever heard you do," I tell her, meaning it.

Charlie pipes up, "What's the catch?"

Winslow shrugs absently, but I see the sparkle in her smile. "He's writing my thesis."

"Typical," Charlie says, rolling her eyes. I bite back a laugh. I haven't seen Charlie quite so snippy with Winslow before and I like it. The girl who threw a glass of champagne in my face has returned.

"We can't all be spoiled princesses, can we?"

Winslow says as the lift comes to a stop, the irony in her words apparently lost on her.

Before I'm able to respond, Winslow is darting off down the mountain in her sleek black attire, and I turn to the cutest marshmallow I've ever wanted to take a bite of.

"I got you," I tell her as she gingerly gets off the lift, taking her time when they stop it for her, much to the annoyance of the people behind her. But I don't care. I glare at them. "Cool it," I snap in their direction. I'm not rushing Charlie into anything.

I want to of course - rush it all. I want to get back together. Not for a hook-up, but for real. I want to confess my love, offer her my heart.

But I know that we need to take things slow.

Baby steps. Bunny slopes.

As I stand waiting for her, Charlie whips past me, laughing as her skis glide through the snow. "Come on, slowpoke," she hollers.

I shake my head in wonder, knowing I'll follow her anywhere she wants to go.

17

CHARLIE

The day could go so many ways - there's a moment before I get off the ski lift, when Winslow zips past us, that I really think I am going to end up at the bottom of the mountain in a marshmallow-y heap.

But then Spencer takes my hand and helps me off the lift, glaring at the people behind us, his gaze not on Winslow in her perfect little ski suit - but on me.

His eyes so full of concern and care and devotion, that it gives a spark of confidence in myself, but also in us. Spencer and I have been through hell and back, and here we are, on the top of the mountain, together.

We can make this work. I want to make this

work. So I forget about messing up and twisting the skis and losing the poles and instead I just have fun.

With the man I am crazy, head over heels for.

The man who patiently waits as I slowly but surely make it down the mountain in one piece.

"You were incredible," he says generously.

"You are so patient with me."

He kisses me then, under the blue skies and bright sun, the white mountains so bright and his gloved hand holding me in place. "You make it easy, Charlie Hayes."

I feel like a princess. His princess. And yes it is cheesy, and I'm certainly not wearing a ball gown and these long skis are definitely not glass slippers, but here, with him, I feel like I'm his princess. Like I am his.

"Should we go up again?" I ask, not because I am trying to be a good sport, but because Spencer was right. I need this. To move my body and fill my lungs with this fresh mountain air - to push aside thoughts of my mom and dad and school and jobs, and just be here, in the moment.

He gives me a wide smile. "God, you make me happy."

The simple truth of it makes me laugh. Reminds me that Spencer Beckett is more than Ivy

League royalty. He is the man that somehow stole my heart.

In the bathroom, I strip out of my wool socks and thermal underwear and slip a thick robe over my shoulders. As I step out of the bathroom, I groan dramatically. "Every muscle aches. Literally, every one."

Spencer has on a robe too and is pouring us glasses of champagne. "Maybe I pushed you too hard?"

I shake my hand, taking the flute he offers me. "No, I'm glad we stayed as long as we did, even if we might pay for it later. It was a lot of fun."

"So you'll come up here with me again?"

I bite the corner of my lip. "Yes, I will. You were a good teacher, Spencer."

"You were a good student." He laces his fingers with mine and gestures outside. "There's a hot tub outside on our private veranda. Might relax your muscles."

"I didn't bring a suit," I say, immediately realizing how dumb that sounds.

He grins. "I think we can manage without."

Spencer steps outside and then turns on the jets to the tub as I grab the bottle of champagne to top off our glasses.

"It's so cold," I say jumping from one foot to the next. "The ground is so cold."

He takes the bottle and glass from my hand, setting them on the side of the tub, then takes my hand and helps me across to the steps. "Easy does it."

I slip off my robe and step into the steaming water. "Oh my god, you've gotta get in here," I moan, turning back to face him. His eyebrows are raised as he watches me sink into the water. "What?"

He looks me over. "You just...you look like..."

"Like what?" I ask, immediately doubting my sense of security. Spencer has been with so many women, so many model-worthy women. Here I am stripping for him without a second thought. Maybe he forgot what I really look like. It's been awhile since we've been together.

"You're so beautiful, Charlie. Sometimes it takes my breath away."

I shake my head, wanting to accept his words, but knowing that right now there is nothing that ties us together beyond our past. We aren't dating, we're...friends. Friends who like to flirt and kiss and get naked.

We aren't just friends. I know that. But what are we?

Spencer sets his robe aside, and steps toward the hot tub. My body tingles - and it's not from the hot water - it's his *everything*. He is so chiseled, a ladder of abs that makes my fingers itch with need. They long to run over him. My eyes move downward, taking in his thickness. My core tightens with want as I watch his perfect form walks toward the steps. His muscles tensing as he moves.

"You don't just take my breath away," I tell him as he climbs in. "You make me forget *how to* breathe."

He smirks. "You want to make me blush?"

I shake my head. "No. That's not what I want."

Our eyes meet and my words hang in the air. He sits opposite me, and I wonder why he didn't pull me into his lap. Why he didn't set me down on his cock and take me here and now.

I want him to.

Instead, he clears his throat. "Can we talk?" he asks.

"Sounds serious," I say, fully aware of how hard

my nipples are, how my clit has begun to throb in anticipation.

"It is."

My brows furrow. "What is it?"

"I want to ask you something, Charlie. And I want you to answer me honestly, without holding back."

"What is it? You can ask me anything, Spencer."

"Would you consider giving us another shot? A real chance. An all in, no second guessing, give it our all, shot?"

I blink. "My body knows what it wants - but that was never the question."

When Spencer and I come together, everything makes sense. Our bodies are in sync, it's like they know the same beat, we're made with the same rhythm.

It's everything else that was our problem. Our families, our futures, our dreams.

His friends, his ex, his fear.

My scholarship status, my job, my insecurity.

"I know last time I let other people get in the way of us, but I won't let that happen again."

"What are you saying?" I ask, moving toward him. Closer, I see the knot of worry in his eyes.

He wants this. Me. He's scared of it not happening.

"Tonight could go a few different ways, Charlie."

I lick my lips, still sitting across from him, but close enough that he could take me in his arms if he wanted.

"How could it go?" I ask.

He pulls me closer, his hand on my neck, drawing me to him. My body pulses with want as his thumb runs over my lips. "We could fuck all night," he tells me. "I could make your pussy so happy. I could get you off until you forget your name. I could make your toes curl and your voice go hoarse."

I close my eyes, wanting all those things so badly. He kisses my ear, his hot breath sending a current of want over me.

"You could sit on my lap, Charlie, right here." He takes my hand and places it on his growing cock. I stroke him, wanting this. His hard length teases me in all the right ways and my poor little pussy is already crying for relief.

"You could ride my cock until your sweet pussy tightens around me, until your tits are bouncing against my chest, until your back arches as you orgasm the way your perfect little body was made to do."

He runs his tongue over my neck, plucking my nipples until I'm whimpering. Already I'm jelly in his hands.

"Or?" I ask, breathlessly.

"Or it could be about more than sex. About more fucking until we pass out."

He pulls me to him, into his lap. It's the place I want to be, and I know he knows it. I close my eyes tighter, scared to look in his eyes because there is only one thing I really want.

A future.

Our future.

"It's okay, Charlie," he says. "You can look at me."

"I'm scared," I say, wrapping my arms around him. Pressing my cheek to his chest. I want this. All of it. And I need him to say it. To want the same thing as me. I'm scared because my heart is his, it wasn't even a choice. It just happened. And the idea of not having his heart in return? It's terrifying.

"Don't be scared, listen." He lifts my chin with his finger, his cock pressed to my belly, my core desperate to be filled. I look at him, hating that I feel both on the verge of tears and ecstasy.

"You're my favorite person to be around," he tells me. "You make me laugh and smile and have hope. I want to go all in with you, Charlie Hayes."

"You do?"

He nods. "So fucking bad."

"What does that mean, exactly?"

"Be my girlfriend."

I lick my lips. "That's what you want?"

"It's all I want."

My chin quivers. "It's all I want too."

"You sure?" He presses my hand to his cock again. "I'm pretty sure I see something else in your eyes."

I laugh, unable to help myself. It's Spencer. My Spencer. The man who makes me crazy and happy and horny all at once.

"So this is happening? We're like, together?" I ask.

He nods, and then he kisses me. It's different than all the kisses that came before. Now we have more than a past, we have the promise of a future.

"I want you to fuck me so bad," I tell him in between kisses. "I want your cock inside me."

"I like it when you talk all dirty," he says, his fingers opening me up. I inhale sharply as my tightness expands for him. My core is already on fire, desperate for him to make me come.

We move together, my body opening as his cock begins to fill me. I'm already so close. I move my hips in a small circle, anxious and greedy. "Oh Spence," I moan, wanting to do more than come. I want to fall. I want to crash.

"You feel so good," he tells me.

And the feeling is more than mutual.

My pussy tightens as he fills me up, as he thrusts deep inside me, as I kiss him harder, our lips parting as we inhale one another.

When we come, it's fierce; it's fire and force and I'm screaming his name.

"Yes, Spence, yes."

I know I'm loud, but I don't care. I'm not just having sex. Right now, my boyfriend is getting me off, and it feels really freaking good.

18

SPENCER

"I wish we could stay one more day," Charlie murmurs against my chest as we lie in bed and watch the sun rise over the ski hill.

I kiss her forehead, drawing her closer to me. "We can if you want."

She sighs. "I do, but I have a paper due, and a quiz on Thursday that I have to study for."

"Have you made any plans for summer vacation yet?" The question has been on my mind for a while now. And since we're really together now, I can't imagine ever being apart.

The idea of spending months without her slays me.

She rolls over, her chin resting on her palms and studies me. "Usually I go home, work as much as I can. But my dad already had an offer on the house so..." She gives a small shrug. "I don't know...probably find a cheap place to rent and see if I can pick up extra shifts at the restaurant." Her brows draw down and a deep worry line forms between them. "I mean if I get into the master's program. It's weird that I haven't heard yet."

"You'll get in." I brush a strand of light brown hair away from her cheek.

"I hope so."

"What about you? Have you decided who you're going to intern with?"

"No." Tension makes my muscles go stiff, because I honestly still have no fucking clue what I'm going to do after I graduate. I know what my parents want me to do, and I've already had offers - good offers. But none that sit right in my gut.

"I guess you still have time to decide."

"I actually did something..." I wince because I'm not sure how she'll take it when I tell her I already got my acceptance into the Ph.D. program last week. I'd applied just for the hell of it, not really thinking about accepting the offer, but now...If she's going to be here at Princeton, it's where I want to be too.

"What?" she asks when I don't continue.

I shift in bed, sitting up. "I was thinking about staying."

"Staying?"

"At Princeton. At least for another four years."

"It's a little late to apply for the doctorate program."

"Yeah." I rub the back of my neck. "Actually, I did already. And I got in."

"Oh. Wow. That's...amazing. Right?"

"You're not upset?" I pull her onto my lap.

"Why would I be upset? So are you going to take it?"

"I haven't decided yet. My parents..." I let out a heavy sigh. "They won't be happy."

"That you'll be a doctor?" She shakes her head. "That's just so...bizarre. But wouldn't having a Ph.D. help in politics?"

"That's the thing, I'm still not sure if I'm headed in that direction. I want to make a difference, but in my own way."

"You're amazing, you know that?"

I chuckle, "Yeah, you told me that a few times last night."

She wraps her arms around my neck and smirks down at me. "When you asked me to be your girlfriend it got me a little … excited."

"Is that what we're calling it?" I ask, remembering the way she orgasmed. It was so loud and so fucking hot that my cock aches at the memory alone. I pull her to me, running my hand over her bare skin. "God, you feel so good."

She licks her lips. "You feel pretty good too." She begins to stroke my shaft, run her fingers over my balls.

"I missed you, Charlie. When we were apart. We can't let that happen again."

She looks up at me, stirring a primal need inside of me. Maybe it's her long lashes and tousled hair, her pouty lips, her wide eyes. But it is more than that. It transcends lust, physical attraction. MY desire to take care of her reaches deep inside me, to my core.

I won't let anything happen to her.

"What is it?" she asks.

I kiss her, hard. My mouth on hers, making a promise. One I don't need to say aloud, but I'm making the vow all the same. I won't let her down. Ever again.

She senses the shift in the mood, my longing to be with her, and she moves down the bed, her tongue running along my length, twirling over my tip where hot cum escapes. She swipes it away with her little pink tongue, and my cock hardens, grows. It knows what it wants. Her.

She takes me in her mouth, fully, sucking me and it's not enough. I need more. Everything. I pull her around, needing her ass in my face, wanting to lick her sweet pussy as she sucks me off.

"Oh Spence," she whimpers as I breathe hot air against her. She begins to move faster, her sucking tight and tender as I squeeze her perfect ass. I lick her, loving her taste, her scent, loving the way she squirms as I mouth-fuck her, making her nice and wet and ready. Her pussy drips for me, but it's my cock that is losing control.

"I'm gonna come, baby," I tell her, and she's pulling away from me. Her hands still on my cock, and when she spins, I can see her face. She pulls my cock from her mouth, my cum flowing from my tip, my release coating her tits, dripping from her nipples. Her desire takes over as she pulls me back in her mouth, sucking me again, my cum sliding down her throat as I finish.

I pull her to me then. "What the hell was that?" I ask, my cock still hard as hell.

"I want to make up for lost time, is all," she says with a sultry smile.

"God, I just won the girlfriend lottery."

She licks her lips. "I love it when you come in my mouth, it makes me …." She rolls over on the bed, her finger against her clit. "Really, really horny."

I move on top of her. "Good, because I'm not finished with you." Watching her touch herself got me good and ready the way nothing else ever has. Her fingers move in tight circles and I ease myself inside her as her fingers keep up the good work.

"I'm so close," she moans, and I know how to get her off even faster. When I fill her up hard and fast, she loses control in the best possible way. My cock enters her tightness, and she gasps, clawing at my back with her nails, her pleasure evident in the way she screams my name.

"Oh, Spence, oh, oh, I'm coming," she whimpers, and I don't need her to tell me to know it's true. Her body shakes as she gets off, the enjoyment written on her face and I pull her to me as I come too. When we finish, we laugh, the morning going way better than I hoped.

"God," I tell her, rolling to face her. "I need to get you away from school more often if that's how you get when you really relax."

She laughs. "I don't know what came over me."

I grin. "I'm pretty sure *I came* all over you."

She giggles, tossing a pillow at me. "You are the naughtiest boy ever."

I pin her to the bed, my cock so fucking greedy I could take her all over again, but my phone starts vibrating on the table beside the bed.

"You should get that," she says, kissing my nose.

"I thought we were gearing up for round two?"

She wraps her legs around me playfully. "I really need to get back to campus and finish that paper."

"You're right," I say as she moves to get out of the bed as I reach for my phone to see who the hell is interrupting some of the best sex of my life. I answer the call as Charlie starts getting dressed. "Hello?"

There's no response for a moment, but when I hear the voice on the other end, my blood goes cold.

Ethan.

"I gave you the fucking money to keep your mouth shut. Don't go having morals on me now. That chick was dead. There was nothing either of us could do. But I swear to God, that if I go down, you'll go down with me."

The same clip begins to repeat itself, and I realize it's a recording.

My day started so fucking perfect … and only

moments later it comes crashing to a halt. I feel sick and I sit on the edge of the bed, trying to concentrate, trying to keep from losing my shit.

"Spencer, what's wrong?" Charlie is beside me, hand on my shoulders and I realize that I've sunk down on the floor, phone trembling against my ear as the recording starts for the third time.

I put it on speaker.

"Who is that?" Charlie asks, one palm on my cheek, worry in her eyes.

"Eth—" I choke on his name. "Ethan."

"Your brother."

All I can do is nod as his voice echoes through the phone. But it's his words that fill me with dread.

I gave you the fucking money to keep your mouth shut. Don't go having morals on me now. That chick was dead. There was nothing either of us could do. But I swear to God, that if I go down, you'll go down with me.

What had he done?

"What does it mean?" Charlie asks, taking the phone from me and ending the torture. But I can see her hands shaking. The terror in her eyes. "Who would send this to you?"

"Someone who wants me to know what he did."

"You think..?" She chews on her bottom lip, dread in her voice. "You think he killed someone?"

I drag my hands through my hair, tugging at it. "It sure as fuck sounded like that." I think back to the last few months before he died. Ethan had always been hard to read, but my brother had become cold, isolated. Had it been guilt that had driven him to drugs and finally over that cliff?

"Jesus," I breathe out. "What am I supposed to do with this?"

"I don't know."

I swallow hard. "I need to go to my parents. If someone is using this to blackmail me or them, then I need to let them know. They wouldn't be the first person after the Beckett money."

My phone pings with a new text.

It's Charlie who reads it first and I see the color drain from her face. She hands me my phone, hands trembling. "I think they want more than just money."

I read the text out loud, "The king already fell, and the prince will too. Last warning. Leave Cinderella alone."

"What the hell?" Charlie rasps out. "Who?"

"I don't know," I say through clenched teeth, cupping her jaw, and wondering if this isn't all tied together with the letters and threats Charlie received, the blog posts, the photographer at the library.

I'm shaking, my body feeling like ice.

"Hey." Her arms are around me. "Whatever this is, we'll figure it out. Maybe what he said was taken out of context. Maybe—"

"Maybe my brother didn't try to bribe someone about a person's death?" I sneer, not knowing how his words can be taken any other way. I know my family has secrets - but this? My brother being a killer? It's too fucking much to take.

"I don't know," she says quietly. "But I think you're right, you do need to tell your parents."

I nod, knowing it's true. My parents need to know. But after our tense conversations over the last week, I hate that this recording is what will bring us together.

CHARLIE OFFERED to go with me to Washington, and while I knew it was selfish of me, I let her, needing her beside me as I face whatever the hell this is.

"You okay?" she asks as we walk up the steps of my parents' house.

"No," I admit, squeezing her hand. "But I'm glad you're with me."

She gives a tight smile. "You've been there for me plenty of times, it's the least I can do."

Except this isn't like her mother's illness, or untimely death. This is about my brother, a man who I idolized, committing a crime that he tried to cover up.

"Spencer?" It's my mother who greets us in the foyer. As usual she's done up like she's about to go to some charity gala, even though it's only early afternoon. And I can smell vermouth on her breath when she hugs me. "What are you doing here?"

I step back and place my arm around Charlie's waist, needing her strength right now. "You haven't met my girlfriend yet? Mom this is Charlotte Hayes."

"Hi, Mrs. Beckett. It's nice to finally meet you." Charlie holds out her hand, but my mom just looks down at it like she's offering her a cup of poison.

"Yes, I've heard a lot about you." My mother's smile is as fake as the blonde highlights that streak her hair.

"Is Dad here?" I ask, looking around the house. It's quiet. Too quiet. And my news is going to stir so much up.

"He's in his office on a call."

"Can you get him? There's something I need to talk to you both about."

My mother looks between Charlie and me, color draining from her cheeks as she obviously comes to her own conclusion about why we're here. Her hand comes to her chest, resting over her heart, and she calls out for one of the waitstaff before sitting down dramatically in one of the antique armchairs in the front parlor room.

Charlie and I follow her, and I whisper in her ear, "I'm pretty sure she thinks you're pregnant."

"Oh my, god." Her eyes go wide. "You have to tell her I'm not."

I chuckle, feeling a small weight lift from me for the first time all day since I got the call. "Not yet."

"You're terrible."

I shrug.

"Yes, ma'am?" A young maid, who must be new to the staff asks as she comes into the room.

"Tell Mr. Beckett that his son and..." My mother glances at Charlie, face ashen. "And his girlfriend are here, and his presence is needed."

The girl nods and starts to leave.

"And bring me a Manhattan, dry..." my mom calls after her. "And make it a double."

"Early in the day to be drinking," I say, raising a brow at her.

She waves her hand at me in disapproval, then changes the subject. "Your father was talking to Carter Madison last night, he said he offered you an internship this summer. It'll be so nice to have you closer to home. We can have more family dinners and—"

"I haven't decided if I'll take it." I usher Charlie to sit in one of the chairs across from my mother but continue to stand myself. I'm feeling restless, and even though I sometimes enjoy watching my mom squirm, I also don't want to cause her any more heartbreak than she's already been through.

I start to doubt whether it was a good idea to invite her into the conversation. Maybe I should have just gone to my father.

"Spencer?" My mother says my name harshly. "I asked who else you were considering."

I frown at her until I realize she's talking about the internship. "Actually, I was thinking about taking the summer off."

Mom's eyes narrow at Charlie. "I suppose this was your idea?"

Charlie lifts her eyebrows. "No. It wasn't. I don't even know what I'm doing this summer."

"Figured as much," Mom says with disapproval. "Waiting to see what opportunities come your way, is that it?"

I clear my throat. "Mother, can we not do this?" Running a hand over my jaw, I add, "Charlie applied for a master's program and is waiting to hear back." I want my mother to know how accomplished my girlfriend is.

"You don't need to explain things for me, Spence," Charlie says. "I don't need to justify anything to—"

My mom cuts her off. "Really darling," she says condescendingly. "Defensive women are rarely attractive."

Charlie's lips curl up at the corners and I am so fucking proud of her iron will. She doesn't need to lower herself to my mother's level. And as soon as we tell my parents the reason we are here, I'm taking my girlfriend away from this hellhole.

"Actually, Mom, I applied for the doctorate program at Princeton. But really, that has nothing to do with why we are here."

There goes her hand again, straight to her heart, and I swear she looks ready to pass out, like I just told her I was thinking about joining the Russian mafia.

When she starts into a lecture, I stop her, "That's not why I came to see you. I have other matters to discuss, but maybe it's best I just speak with Dad."

"Whatever you need to tell him, you can say to me." Tears are in her eyes now as she looks at Charlie with a mix of disgust and horror. "Please tell me you didn't let that—"

"Careful, Mother," I warn, but it's already too late, the woman has gotten herself in hysterics.

I shouldn't have brought Charlie here.

"How could you be so stupid?" my mother says. "All your life I warned you that there would be...*girls* like that who would try and trap you—"

"Charlie isn't pregnant, mother."

My father coughs from the entrance to the parlor. "Good to know," he says blandly.

"But if you say another word against her, I'll walk out that door—"

"No need for dramatics," my father says, walking across the room and taking Charlie's hand. "It's nice to finally meet you, Ms. Hayes."

Charlie gives him a small smile. "Thank you."

My mom opens and shuts her mouth, but thankfully remains quiet.

"What's all this fuss about?" he asks as he turns to face me.

I shove my hands in my pocket and start to pace. "I got a call this morning."

"Would you like to elaborate," my father says when I don't continue.

"It was a recording of Ethan." I catch the look my parents share, but I don't know what it means. "He was confessing something to someone. Something about paying them off to stay silent. About a dead girl..."

I expect a reaction. Anything. Denial. Yelling. Tears. But I get nothing.

My father sits down heavily, and my mother looks even worse than when she thought Charlie might be pregnant.

And then it hits me.

"You guys know."

My mom winces and my dad won't meet my gaze.

"Shit." It feels like the air has been punched from my lungs. "Whatever it is he did, you guys knew about it. For how long?"

"There's nothing to know," my father says, standing, already collecting himself, emotion void from his voice. "Give me your phone, son.

Whoever sent you the recording will be dealt with."

I shake my head. "Did he kill someone? Did you try and hide it? Jesus, how fucking corrupt is this family?"

"Watch your tone." My father is in front of me, eyes blue steel and all business. "Your brother was a good man. There was an accident. That's all you need to know."

"An accident that you helped him cover up." I say the words, knowing they're the truth.

"You need to be very careful with what you say right now, son."

I know what he's implying. He's worried because Charlie is in the room. Worried about his reputation. Maybe more. Whatever this is, could be criminal.

"Do you know who would send this?" I ask, knowing there's no chance in hell I'm giving him my phone. I don't trust him not to try and sweep this under the hypothetical rug too. But this time, whoever is threatening my family is also threatening Charlie. "If you do you need to tell me. Now."

My father places a hand on my shoulder, and I shrug it off. "I don't. But I'll have my men look into it. Was there anything else?"

I think about telling him about the text but stop myself. "We need to go." I reach for Charlie's hand and start out the door.

"Spencer." My father stops us in the foyer. "You need to let this go. Let me take care of it."

I grunt. "Is that what you said to Ethan?" My lip curls up in a sneer. "That you'd take care of it? And how did that work out? He drove his fucking car off a cliff, because you took care of it—"

The slap echoes through the two-story room, and my cheek is instantly on fire. It's not the first time my father has hit me, but it will be the last. I hear Charlie's sharp intake of breath, and it's the only thing stopping me from striking back.

"Goodbye, Dad," I say before turning and walking out the door with Charlie pressed against me.

I'm still shaking three hours later when we arrive back at Charlie's dorm. Like the ride home, the walk up to her room is filled with tense silence.

I pull her to me when we're in front of her door, and press my forehead to hers, breathing her in, and apologize again, "I'm sorry you had to hear all that."

Her hands cup my jaw and she looks up at me,

concern pulsing in her eyes. "I can handle your parents. I'm just worried about you."

"Once I find out who's behind this, I'll be a lot better."

Charlie opens her door, and Daphne is there with her purse in hand. "I thought I heard voices." She smiles, but it seems fake. "Did you two have a nice weekend?"

Charlie nods. "There were some really great moments," she says softly. "Some not as great."

Daphne cocks her head to the side. "Okay...a little cryptic. Care to elaborate?"

Charlie shakes her head, setting her duffel bag on her bed. "Not tonight. It's been a long day and I have a paper to finish."

"I'm headed to the dining hall. Want anything?" she asks, pretty much ignoring me.

"No thanks," Charlie says, massaging her neck as Daphne leaves. At least her roommate recognizes that Charlie isn't in the mood for conversation.

"You going to be okay tonight?" I ask, stepping closer. "You can always come to my place if you want."

"Sounds nice, but if I go with you, I won't get my work done." She sighs, pressing her palms to my chest. "Do you ever wish we could just rewind? Stay in a happy moment, forever?"

I nod, tucking a loose strand of hair behind her ear. "What would your moment be?"

She lifts her chin, those hazel eyes meeting mine and sending a much-needed jolt of heat to my heart. "Last night when you asked me to be your girlfriend was pretty good."

"Last night was perfect."

She stands on her tiptoes and kisses me. "Thank you," she says.

"For what? You're the one who has been my rock all day."

She kisses me again, quickly this time. "No, I mean, thank you for trusting me. For letting me into your heart."

My hands cup her face. I kiss her nose. Her cheeks. "You're not going anywhere, Charlie Hayes. We're officially together now, that means something to me."

"It means something to me too." She smiles, her cheeks rosy and so damn cute I pinch them. "It means you need to walk me to my lecture tomorrow morning. Maybe write me little notes and pass them to me in between classes. Make me a playlist. Take me on a long drive so we can make out in the car. You know, boyfriend things."

I chuckle. "Wow, a lot of responsibilities I didn't know about. And what will you do for me?"

She wraps her arms around me. "Oh, don't you worry, Princeton Charming. I take my girlfriend duties seriously," she whispers in my ear. "I'm planning on kneeling before your throne. Maybe polishing your crown?"

Then she laughs, slapping my butt as she ushers me out of her room.

19

CHARLIE

Whoever called Spencer and left the text was smart enough to use a burner phone. A week later and we're no closer to tracking the person down. But at least there hasn't been any more calls or texts, and after the news I got today, it's the last thing on my mind.

"I got in," I squeal, not caring that I sound like an adolescent girl.

"What?" Daphne asks, taking her headphones off and putting her laptop to the side as I come bouncing into the room.

"I got accepted to the master's program with a full scholarship," I say breathlessly, still unable to believe it.

"Of course you did." She takes the letter from my hands and scans it. "You're Charlotte Hayes."

I don't even let the small bite of jealousy I hear in her voice bother me. I'm on the phone to my dad, to Jill, and then to Spencer.

"I'm so proud of you," Spencer says. "We have to celebrate."

"Yeah." The grin that pulls at my lips hurts my face, but I can't stop smiling. This is what I've worked my ass off for.

"Yates has been bugging me to do a double date with him and Georgia, he suggested Winberie's tonight, but I can tell him we'll do it another night."

"No, that'll be fun. Maybe..." I hesitate, contemplating what I'm about to suggest. "What about inviting Ava and Prescott?"

"You're kidding, right?"

"How long has it been since you talked to either of them? She's your sister and he's..."

"The backstabbing asshole who's screwing my sister."

I sigh. "Yeah, but he's still your oldest friend, even if he is a douchebag. And I saw them together on campus yesterday, they looked...cute and happy."

Spencer groans. "You're a way better person than I am, you know that?"

"Pretty sure we established that a long time ago," I tease.

"Okay, fine, I'll call them. And I'll pick you up at eight. Do you want to invite Jill or Daphne?"

I glance over at my roommate who's gone back to sulking on her bed, Beats pulled back over her ears, glowering at whatever she's reading on her laptop.

"No. I think that's enough drama with Ava and Prescott. Just promise me you won't throw any punches."

He chuckles. "Not sure I can do that."

"Spencer."

"Fine. I'll be civil. For you."

"Thank you. I—" Almost say those three words that haven't been spoken out loud, but clamp my mouth over them. I love him. And I think he loves me. But it just hasn't come up, and maybe it's just me being stubborn, but I don't want to be the first to say it. "I'll see you at eight."

After I've hung up, I glance over at Daphne. "Hey, you all right?"

She ignores me even though I know she can hear me. Her moods have been crazy these past couple of weeks. One second she seems fine, the next she's in tears, and the next she's laughing hysterically for no good reason.

I've wondered if maybe she's on something, but if she is I've never seen her take it.

"Okay well, I'm going out tonight to celebrate."

She rips off her headphones. "Thanks for the invite. Have *so* much fun with your new besties."

"Look, I'm not trying to start anything. It's not like you even like Spencer."

She sits up on her bed, crossing her arms. "How do you know?"

"Because whenever he's around, you get a little...territorial."

She rolls her eyes. "Whatever. I already have plans."

I frown. "You do?"

"Yeah," she says, moving from the bed and pulling open her wardrobe. "I have a study date."

"With who?"

She whips around, her eyes haughtily on mine. "With Tatum."

I raise an eyebrow. "With *my* Tatum?" The moment I say it, I know it's wrong. For a hundred different reasons. He isn't mine. He wanted to be, and I told him no and I broke his heart more than once.

"He isn't your property, Charlotte." She scoffs, and annoyance fills her eyes. Annoyance with me. "God, that's kind of your issue, isn't it? The world has to revolve around you."

I run a hand through my hair. "That's not true. I never—"

"What? Never took for granted the fact Tatum is your most loyal friend? Or never took for granted the fact that I am always here for you? For being such a sweetheart you can be kind of a bitch."

My jaw drops. In all this time we've lived together, Daphne has never gone off on me. We've never even fought, not really. "How long have you felt this way?"

Daphne waves her hands in the air. "Whatever, it doesn't matter. You don't seem to care what Tatum thinks anyway."

"You spoke to Tatum about me?"

She shrugs, pushing around her hangers of designer clothing. "It came up once or twice. I mean, the poor guy has been coming around looking for you, but you're never here." She spins to face me. "But I am."

Heat rises to my cheeks. I haven't made time to

hang out with Tatum one on one for weeks. I've hardly seen Jill either. Between work and school and Spence, I'm spread pretty thin. It doesn't make it right, though.

"I'm really sorry Daphne. I wish I'd have known you felt like this. Between my mom and Spence, I've just kind of been MIA."

Daphne sighs. "I know, Charlotte." She sets a hand on my shoulder. "You've had a shitty start to the year. I shouldn't pile it on."

"No, it's good to know where you're coming from. And of course I want you and Tatum to be friends. You are both really generous, I can see why you'd get along."

Daphne flings her arms around me and gives me a hug. "Awww, I love you, Char."

We step apart and I tell her I've got to get ready for tonight, and she's grabbing her books anyway, pushing them in her messenger bag and heading out the door.

"I'll tell Tatum you said hi, okay?" she says with a wave.

I hate that there is a bubble of emotion in me, one I can't quite place. It's not that I'm jealous of Tatum and Daphne hanging out. I want my friends to be happy.

I reach for my phone and send Tatum a quick text.

Me: Maybe we can hang out next week?

Tatum: Sounds great. Miss you C!! Jill, you and me Wednesday wings?

I give him a thumbs up and drop my phone on my bed, feeling less unsettled about Tatum and me.

Daphne may have stirred up some negative emotions, but right now, I'm not going to let any of them get in my way.

I've been accepted to the master's program, and tonight, it's my turn to celebrate.

THE RESTAURANT IS PACKED, but I'm not here with some random college guy. I'm here with Spencer Beckett. A hostess leads us past the crowded tables and ushers us to a back table that is sectioned off from the rest of the restaurant.

Everyone else is already here, and Ava stands to give me a hug, and Georgia and I exchange hellos. It's the first time Spencer and I have been out on a group date and it feels awkward - in a good way. Prescott is grinning as he claps Spencer on the back.

I squeeze Spencer's hand as we sit. I know he must recognize the rough edges fading from his oldest friend's face. Ava is a good match for him, even if it is unexpected.

"I ordered bottles of red and white, wasn't sure what you drink, Charlotte," Yates says.

"White, please," I say. Settling into my chair and taking in the company. They are all so posh, so refined. When it's just Spencer and me, I forget that we come from different worlds, but sitting here with Georgia and Ava, I'm reminded just how different I am from the Princeton Elite.

"We should toast to Charlotte," Prescott says, giving me a genuine smile and lifting his glass of red wine. "For getting into the master's program."

My cheeks warm. "Oh, no, everyone here is so accomplished." I know for a fact Georgia was also recently accepted into grad school. Yates is going to Harvard Law in the fall and Ava was recently granted a summer internship at a fashion house in London.

"Then to all of us," Prescott says, taking my cue. "To our futures."

We clink glasses and I'm glad the attention was taken off me. I'm proud of myself, but I know that in the big picture, my accomplishments haven't added up to as much as some people at this table.

"I heard you guys went skiing recently?" Georgia says, her finger running across her pearl necklace.

"Yeah, it was pretty spectacular. It was Charlie's first time, but you wouldn't have guessed it." Spencer places an arm over the back of my chair, and his eyes sparkle with something that looks like pride.

"First time?" Ava's jaw drops. "That's crazy. I swear our parents forced us on the slopes when we were toddlers." She shivers. "I always hated the cold. But Switzerland has the best chalets. You have to have Spencer take you there, and the chocolate is to die for."

I give her a small smile, not about to admit that I've never actually left North America.

"Remember that trip we took to Whistler?" Georgia asks, looking around the table. "Was that winter break of sophomore year?"

"Of college?" I ask.

"No, high school," Prescott says, refilling Ava's glass. "I remember we didn't have our driver's licenses yet and we got so pissed that we couldn't rent snowmobiles."

The table starts reminiscing about the long forgotten weekend, and I sip my wine, thinking about my own sophomore winter break. I was probably marathoning Harry Potter and making sugar cookies. Nothing like elaborate ski trips out of the country.

"You've all been friends a long time then?" I ask after we've ordered.

"Forever," Yates says, setting his arm around Georgia. "It's kind of amazing. All those trips and vacations as friends and now..."

"Now we're planning a trip to Europe - just the two of us," Georgia says with a smile, snuggling closer to Yates, her smile infectious. "No friends, no family. Just us."

"That's really romantic," I say, admiring the two of them. "You have so much history."

They laugh and exchange a look, one that holds a silent conversation.

"Sometimes though, it's a bad thing," Georgia admits. "I went through a lot of phases I'd maybe prefer my boyfriend to not remember."

"Like the summer you were obsessed with Twilight," Prescott teases.

"Hey, Ava has seen you at your worst too,"

Georgia tosses back. "Remember when you bleached your hair?"

"No one could forget Prescott's frosted tips," Ava laughs. "Though, I suppose he saw me when I was fangirling over One Direction."

"We've all been there," I say with a smile. "Though was more of a Bieber girl myself."

Spencer's jaw drops. "Really? You have impeccable taste in music and yet you had Bieber Fever?"

I shrug. "What can I say, I had a thing for the heartthrob who looks like the boy next door."

The table laughs, and I ask Spencer, "So now you know I was a *Belieber*, what was your most embarrassing phase?"

The table starts to discuss Spencer's past with animation.

Prescott tosses out, "Maybe the time he decided to wear Hawaiian shirts all summer?"

"Oh my god, Winslow refused to go in public with him," Georgia says. Then she cringes, glancing my way. "Sorry, is that awkward to say?"

I shake my head laughing. "Not at all. But I bet there was something more embarrassing than his clothing."

Yates laughs. "No, Spencer tried on lots of looks before landing on this Princeton Charming thing. I still can't block out the memory of his fedora and pinstripe suits."

Ava snorts. "And remember the goth phase? I remember once, he borrowed my black eyeliner."

Spencer laughs. "That was for a joke."

Yates chuckles. "No one was laughing bro."

By the time the waitress brings us dessert, everyone is relaxed and even Spencer and Prescott seem to be getting along.

"So you're headed to Europe this summer?" Spencer asks Yates and Georgia. "That's going to be incredible."

"Yeah, France mostly." Georgia lights up. "I'm a total history nerd," she says in my direction. "And Yates and I are going to visit all the famous Napoleon landmarks."

"What about you guys?" Yates asks Spencer and Prescott. "Any D.C. internships in the works?"

Prescott grins. "Actually, yeah. I'm headed there to work with Robert Claymount in June."

There are a few murmurs of approval and light discussion about the man's politics before Yates directs his question back to Spencer, "And what about you?"

Spencer's brows furrow. "I haven't decided. Lots of options still."

I sip my wine, surprised he is keeping his Ph.D. plans to himself still. I wonder if Ava knows or if his parents haven't disclosed that yet.

"Well, I'm glad I'm not dating a future politician," Georgia laughs. "I can't imagine always having to cross my t's and dot my i's."

Ava nods, looking at me. "Yeah, pressure much, right?"

"Right," I say, glancing over at Spencer's chiseled jaw, wondering just what my boyfriend is thinking.

BACK AT HIS PLACE, Spencer and I quickly undress. "I've wanted to get you out of this dress for hours," he says, pulling it over my head. "I wanted to congratulate you properly."

"And I need to be naked for that?" I ask teasingly.

"Yes." Spencer lifts me up from the floor, making me yelp. "On your back, knees spread."

I nibble at his ear. "I like the sound of that."

He tosses me playfully on his bed. "Then you're really gonna like the sound of this." He dips his head between my legs, his tongue gliding over me. I suck in a deep breath, my body already pulsing with heat.

"Oh God," I moan as Spencer runs a hand over my belly, holding my breast. His other hand massages my inner thigh as his tongue works my clit. "Oh," I moan, sinking into the mattress.

"You taste so good," he says, and I close my eyes, savoring the sensation of his mouth against my skin.

"Oh Spence," I whimper, needing more - wanting everything. "Come here," I plead. "I want you closer."

"Closer than your pussy?" he asks with a smile as he leans over me.

"Yeah," I say as I take hold of his thickness. Loving the way he pulses in my hand, his need for me as obvious as mine for him. "I want this to last forever."

He looks down at me, and I know he realizes I'm talking about more than sex. I'm talking about us.

His hand cups my cheek and he kisses me slowly. So slowly that we both melt into the bed, our bodies wrapped around one another, our hearts beating in a steady rhythm. Not too fast, not too slow. When it's just us, it's just right.

"I want it to last forever, too," he tells me as he eases his cock inside me. Spencer and I lock eyes as we move together, our skin hot and breath shallow.

I gasp as he fills me up, my body still getting used to a man being inside of me. His eyes shine as I whimper the deeper he goes, and I know he loves the fact that he is my first.

My only.

And God, how I love it too.

20

SPENCER

Just admit that you love her. The thought beats through me wildly, almost having a life of its own. Like if I don't say the words, I might explode.

Our breaths are still ragged and rough, our bodies still covered in sweat. I close my eyes, breathing her in, feeling her in every cell of my body. Shit, I'm only twenty-three, I shouldn't be having the thoughts I am.

Of a future.

A family.

A life with her and me and maybe one day children of our own.

I want it all.

Her palm rests on my cheek and when I open

my eyes, she's watching me. "Tell me what you're thinking."

"You'll think it's corny."

She chuckles. "That's one of the things I love about you." She catches her bottom lip between her teeth, and I know she realizes the implication of the words.

"So what are the other things?" I ask, dragging my thumb over her bottom lip until she releases it. "That you love about me."

Her tongue darts out, and I see the teasing in her eyes. "Well, you're a pretty good kisser."

I cock a brow. "Only pretty good?"

She shrugs. "I just think we need to practice more."

"Can't get enough, huh?"

"Of you? Never."

My chest squeezes and I cup her jaw. "I love you, Charlotte Hayes."

Her mouth opens as she sucks in a small breath. "Spence—"

"Want to know why?" I ask.

Her eyes are wide, filled with so much emotion, and she gives a small nod.

"I love you because when you smile the whole room lights up." I press two kisses to her lips. "I love you because when you look at me, I feel like a better man." Shifting slightly, I kiss her eyelids. "I love you because you challenge me, and make me believe in the good in people, in the good in myself." I lower myself and kiss her neck, then meet her intense gaze. "I love you because you're Charlie Hayes, and there's no one in this world like you."

Her bottom lip quivers, but she smiles, and there it is - light.

I tangle my fingers in her hair. "I want forever with you. I know we've had a lot of shit thrown at us, and I'm not sure what tomorrow will bring, but I know we can conquer anything together. You and me against the world. What do you say?"

"I love you, too." A tear slips over her cheek and I kiss it away. "I've wanted to say it for a long time."

I kiss her hard then, our bodies melting into each other. And it's not long before I'm buried inside of her again.

This time it's different though, it's like a barrier has been lifted. Those three simple words bring us closer together.

I love you.

God, it feels so good to say - so good to hear.

"You're smiling so big right now," she tells me as she rolls over, straddling me. Her perfect tits and her smooth skin and that laugh of hers that fills a room. How the hell did I manage to get this woman to see past my thousand flaws and still choose me?

"I'm really fucking happy," I admit as she sinks down on my cock. She leans over, kissing my cheeks, my nose, my lips. She is so tight, still so innocent, and I love that I'm the only man who has ever explored every inch of her skin.

"I'm crazy happy too," she says. "But we need some music. Something romantic?"

"Demanding," I tease, reaching for my phone as she begins to move her hips in a circle. "How's this?"

The song "I Wanna Sex You Up" starts blaring from my surround sound speakers and Charlie starts laughing, her hands on my chest as her shoulders shake. "Nothing says I love you like Color Me Badd."

I sit up, my hands around her waist, and pull her into my lap. "I fucking love you, Charlie Hayes."

Our foreheads touch and we move as one. Her body shaking when the orgasm washes over her, and I'm here, holding her tight. "Oh Spencer," she moans as her body presses tight against mine.

I come deep inside her, then, our lips crashing together; it's impossible to satisfy our need.

So we don't try. Instead, we roll in the tangle of sheets, our hearts one.

Later, my cell buzzes from somewhere in the room, but I ignore it. When Charlie's starts ringing right after, we both frown, and she starts to reach for hers.

"Hello?" Her frown deepens. "Yeah, he's right here. One second." She hands me her phone. "It's Prescott. He sounds upset."

"What's going on?"

"Someone broke into Ava's dorm room when we were out." Prescott is barely holding back his rage, I can hear him ready to snap. "Didn't look like they took anything, but..."

"Tell me."

"The room was covered in blood."

"Blood?"

"Most likely fake or pig's blood. Fuck," he curses, sounding raw, and ready to murder someone. "Ava was traumatized. She was still shaking when I left."

"Shit." I sit up, feeling Charlie's worried gaze on me. "Where's she now?"

"I just dropped her off at my place. I'm going back to talk to campus police, and get some of her things. I got her out of there pretty quickly, so she didn't get a chance to—"

"Pick me up on your way."

"I can deal with it myself."

"Campus police aren't going to do shit? And if this is linked to…" I drag my hands through my hair, then stand and head toward my closet, grabbing the first shirt I see.

"To what?" Prescott demands. "Is there something going on you're not telling me about?"

"You already know about the stuff with Charlie, but there's more since we last spoke."

I fill Prescott in on the voice mail from Ethan, how it was connected to a burner phone, and even though it is hard to admit that my brother was obviously involved in some sketchy shit, the idea of anything happening to my little sister is unbearable.

Fuck family secrets - I have Ava and Charlie to protect.

"Shit, Spencer. Ava is going to be wrecked."

"Less so if she is alive. We have to find whoever is threatening the people I love."

Love.

It's good Charlie knows I'm all in, committed to us. Especially now when someone is so intent on ruining my life.

"You think it's the same person?" Prescott asks.

"I don't know, but I'm sure as hell going to find out."

Prescott's breathing is rough. "There's something else. I got Ava out of the room before she saw it, but…There was something written on the wall in blood."

"What?" I ask through gritted teeth.

"*Royalty must pay*. I'm not sure what it means—"

"I think I do. Or at least I have my suspicions."

"This is really fucked up, Beckett."

"No shit." I glance over at Charlie, my protector mode at full throttle.

"I'm five minutes from your place."

"I'll be ready." I hang up and pull on a pair of jeans, then grab my wallet off the dresser.

"What's going on?" Charlie has already gotten dressed and is chewing on her thumbnail, sitting on the bed, knees tucked under her chin.

God, we've had such a good night, and I don't want to worry her, but I promised no more secrets.

"Someone vandalized Ava's dorm room." I move toward her and hand her phone back.

"Oh no. Is she okay?"

"She's fine. But Prescott and I are going to go and see if we can get some answers."

"Do you want me to come?"

I lean down and press a kiss to her forehead. "No. Stay here. I'll call you."

She grabs my hand as I start to walk away. "I love you."

I inhale, heart swelling despite the fury I feel, but before I leave, I kiss her again, hard, and say with every ounce of my being, "I love you, too."

21

CHARLIE

It's hard to sit still and not pace while I wait to hear back from Spencer. I'm not close to Ava, I don't even have her number on my phone, but I understand probably better than most people what she's going through.

I turn on the TV and flip through a few channels, but I can't concentrate, and I can't help but think this is all about me. Or at least somehow connected to the person who sent me the notes, warning me off Spencer.

But as much as I try to put the pieces together, nothing makes sense. All I know for certain is that someone doesn't want Spencer and me together. But why bring Ava into it? And what does Spencer's brother have to do with it all?

I've chewed my thumbnail down to the skin when I finally stand and turn the TV off, then go back upstairs and check my messages.

There are twelve missed calls from Daphne and a stream of frantic texts. An unsettling feeling washes over me and my skin prickles with premonition as I press the call back button without listening to her messages.

"Charlie you have to come back now," Daphne cries into the phone, her words barely audible through her sobs. "Everything...it's...all...ruined..."

"Calm down. Tell me what happened."

I can hear people in the background. Girls crying, talking animatedly, some yelling so that I can barely hear Daphne.

"Daphne. What's going on?"

"The whole room is ruined. All my clothes...my brand new Versace dress...." She lets out a wailing cry, so loud I have to pull the phone away from my ear.

"I can't understand you."

She keeps sobbing but manages to say one word that sends ice throughout my entire body. "Blood."

"No." Oh my god.

"It's everywhere." Daphne is whimpering now,

and I can hear someone in the background comforting her. "My laptop, my bed..."

"Did you call the campus police?"

"I...think..." She sniffles. "I think someone did. What am I going to do?"

I glance around the bedroom and find Spencer's keys. Prescott picked him up, and I know he won't mind me borrowing the Mercedes to pick Daphne up.

"I'll be there soon. You can come back to Spencer's with me until we figure out who did this."

"You're sure?"

I chew on my bottom lip. I know Daphne and Spencer have never really cared for each other, but I know he'll be okay with her staying here, at least for the night.

"Yeah."

She sucks in a shaky breath. "Okay."

As soon as I hang up, I call Spencer, but it goes straight to voicemail.

"Hey," I say to the machine as I gather my purse, jacket, and boots, and try not to let the anxiety I'm feeling, the sickness at what's been done, come out in my words. I try to remind myself that whatever is ruined, it's just stuff, and stuff can be replaced. "I just got a call from Daphne and whoever vandalized Ava's room, also got to ours..." My stomach rolls thinking about it, not knowing what I'll find when I get there. "So, I hope you're okay with this, but I'm going to take your car and pick Daphne up and bring her back here."

I shrug my jacket on, wishing I was talking to Spencer and not his machine. I need him now. But so does Ava, so I try to sound calm despite the tsunami of emotions that rage inside me.

"Call me back when you get the chance."

After I hang up, I lock the front door before finding Spencer's Mercedes. I've driven it a couple times, but as I pull out of the driveway, my fingers tingle and I feel a weird pressure on the base of my skull, like something isn't right.

"I'm just being paranoid," I mumble to myself, turning on the radio.

But as I make a right, then a left, I notice a set of headlights behind me, following too close. When the road turns into four lanes, I slow to the minimum speed limit, hoping they'll go around me, but they stay on my bumper.

I let out a shaky breath. "It's just someone being an asshole."

When my phone starts ringing, I jump and swerve a little. At the same time the car behind me accelerates and races by me, the tail lights disappearing into the distance.

I glance down at my phone briefly and see the picture of Spencer and me from New Year's Eve that I made as his ID. My phone isn't paired with his car, so I press speaker and accept the call.

"Hey," I say. "You got my message."

"Shit, Charlie." Anger vibrates from his words. "I'm going to find the fucker who did this. I promise you."

"I know."

"Where are you now?"

"Just driving back to the dorm. Daphne's a mess. I hope you don't mind that I invited her back."

"Of course not. I'll meet you there and we'll go home together. How are you holding up?"

My hands are shaking as I turn onto one of the side streets that leads toward campus, but it's not the time to break down.

"I just need to see what I can salvage." A lump grows in my throat as I think about all the mementos I have in the room. Things of little value to anyone else, but to me mean the world. Photo albums, the quilt my grandmother made me when I was ten, the stuffed gorilla I got when my mom took me to the Detroit Zoo when I was eight.

Anger overrides all other emotions.

"I'm just pissed."

"Yeah, I know. But there's one good thing that'll come out of it."

I grunt. "What's that."

"I get to keep you at my place all night."

I can't help but laugh. "Hate to burst your bubble, but remember Daphne comes with me."

He groans. "Right. Any way we can pawn her off on Tatum. You said they're getting closer."

I chuckle. "You're still jealous of him."

"Nah. I've got your heart, Hayes. Nothing and no one can take that away."

"You know I love how corny you are." I frown when I look in my rearview mirror and see a car speeding toward me. It's dark, so I'm probably wrong, but it looks like the same car from before.

Like Tatum's car.

"Charlie?" Spencer's voice echoes through the car. "You still there?"

"Uh, yeah...Did you say something?"

"What's wrong?"

"Nothing." The car speeds up, flashing its high

beams and getting right on my bumper, then slowing down again. "What the fuck."

"Charlie, talk to me."

"I don't know. There's a car..." I don't tell him that it's the same make and model as Tatum's. Again, it's dark, and he's not the only person in Princeton who drives a beat-up Ford Taurus.

But the silhouette is definitely a man.

The car speeds up again, this time blaring its horn before squealing its tires right before it hits me, and taking a sharp left.

"What the fuck is going on?" Spencer shouts.

"There was someone on my bumper, but they're gone."

He curses under his breath before asking, "How far away are you."

I glance around, not knowing this area well. "I think fifteen minutes."

"Okay, just drive safe and don't stop. I'll meet you in front of your dorm."

"You're a good boyfriend, Princeton Charming," I say teasingly, trying to lighten the mood, or maybe as a way to try to calm my own nerves. "I think you deserve a—"

The Taurus pulls out in front of me, and in order not to hit him, I have to slam my brakes, but I must catch a piece of black ice, because the car starts spinning.

Everything happens so fast, and yet it seems like slow motion. I try my best to straighten the car, but I see the tree in the corner of my vision seconds before I hear the crunching of metal and Spencer shouting at me through the speaker on my phone.

Glass shatters around me, and I feel something sharp in my side, and something warm running down my face. The airbag must've gone off, even though I don't remember it, because it's still slightly inflated in front of me.

"Charlie," Spencer yells, but his voice is muffled. My phone has fallen on the passenger side floor and when I try to reach for it, I let out a cry of pain.

I glance down at my stomach and see dark red blood staining my shirt. "Oh god."

"Christ, Charlie, talk to me."

Bile rises in my throat, and my vision goes blurry. Headlights beam in front of me, and a tall figure walks toward the car. I can only see the man's silhouette. Tall, muscular, the guy has on an old baseball cap pulled low, and wearing a Princeton Athletics sweatshirt.

I blink trying to make the guy come into focus,

but my head feels fuzzy, my vision like I'm underwater.

"Fuck," I hear the guy mutter before he starts pacing outside of my car.

"Tatum?" My voice is weak. I don't want to believe it's him, but I recognize the stain on the back of the sweatshirt where I accidentally spilled bleach when I'd been doing his laundry.

"Is Tatum with you?" Spencer yells through the phone. "Charlie, answer me right now. What was that sound."

And then the guy is walking away, he gets into the car and slams the door, before speeding in reverse. My brain must not be working, because in no reality does any of this make sense. And I'm so damn cold.

"Help," it's all I can say as the world starts to grow farther away, like I'm being sucked backward through a black tunnel.

"Okay." Fear strains Spencer's words. "I going to find someone with a phone to call an ambulance, because I'm not getting off this call, understand?"

I whimper, but the pain is somewhat bearable now. I just feel tired. So damn tired.

Spencer is yelling at someone else now, barking orders. I don't know how much time passes, but I'm pretty sure I lost consciousness for a moment, because I can hear sirens in the distance, and Spencer shouting my name.

"Spencer," I mumble, unable to open my eyes.

"Yeah," he says, voice ragged with emotion. "I'm here. I've called an ambulance. There's GPS on my car, so they should be there soon. Just stay with me okay?"

"I'm sorry..."

"For what?"

"I...wrecked...your car."

"I don't give a fuck about the car, Charlie. I just need to know you're okay."

Ice flows through my veins and my body feels heavy. Is this what it feels like to die?

There's shouting outside the car, and when I manage to open my eyes slightly, I see flashes of blue and red around me.

"They're...here..."

"Okay, good," Spencer says. "I'm going to meet you at the hospital. You're going to be all right."

Except I don't know if I am. And when I close my eyes again, it isn't darkness but light I see. Someone pulling me, warmth surrounding me, and I want to let it, because I know it's where my mom is. I miss her so much ... and now she's here. With me.

And I'm not sure I have the strength to fight my way back to the cold, icy reality.

So I do the only thing I can, I let the light consume me.

22

SPENCER

"You need to calm the hell down." Prescott is in my face, his hands on my shoulders, shaking me. "Charlie's going to be fine, but you need to keep your head."

"She sounded bad, man." I heard the paramedics working on her, heard the words they used, slow pulse, possible internal bleeding, head trauma, before they took her away. I can't breathe, can't move. It feels like the whole goddamn world has fallen out beneath my feet. One minute we are confessing our love and the next, our entire world is falling apart.

I can't lose her.

"We need to go, now." Prescott thankfully has

kept his cool, and I'm grateful for him when he forces me to move.

I tug at my hair when we're in his car, racing through red lights toward the hospital. I can hear sirens and wonder if it's the ambulance Charlie is in.

"Drive faster," I bark out, before letting out a stream of curses.

"You need to keep your head, Beckett." He glances over at me, features tight. "Whatever happens you can't let her see you like this."

"How the fuck am I supposed to be?" I punch the dashboard, hard enough that I feel something snap in my fist. But I welcome the pain - need it.

"Does she have anyone you need to call?" Prescott asks, voice steady.

"Her dad. Shit. He just lost his wife. I can't..." I run my hands over my face. "Can't be the one who tells him."

"All you're going to tell him is that she's been in an accident. That's all you know. She might be sitting up, smiling when we get there."

I nod, wanting to believe him, before I find Daniel Hayes' number on my phone.

"Spencer?" he says when he answers.

"Shit." Words are stuck in my throat.

"What's wrong."

I swallow past the enormous lump in my throat and try to man up, but I do a pretty shitty job of it when I choke out, "Charlie's been in a car accident. They're taking her to the hospital right now..." I swallow the emotions that threaten to overwhelm me.

"Is she...Is she all right?"

"I don't know." I take a steadying breath and focus. "I'm going to make a call, someone will be at your place soon to pick you up and bring you here."

I make the required calls, to Jill, Daphne, and when I end the one with my sister Ava, Prescott is pulling the car to the curb outside of the emergency room.

Nothing matters but Charlie, and I know I raise a few eyebrows as I push my way through the line, demanding the nurse at the front desk tell me where they've taken her. When the gray-haired woman only sneers at me, Prescott steps in. I pace while he talks to her, and I'm not sure what he says, but it works, and a few seconds later we're being escorted through the double doors to a small, private waiting room.

"What the hell is this?" I demand.

The male nurse who ushered us back here gives

me a hard look, but I see sympathy in his eyes, and I want to hit him for it. "Someone will be in shortly to talk to you."

"Talk to me about what?" I yell.

Prescott steps in front of me when I move to follow the nurse out of the room. "Cool it, man. I asked them to give us a private room while we wait."

"I don't want to fucking wait. I need to see her."

"What you need is to let the doctors do their job."

I sit down heavily in one of the plastic covered chairs and let the deep groan I've been holding back rip from my chest.

Prescott sits across from me, knees on his thighs, and I know he wants to say something.

"What?"

"This wasn't just an accident," he says, voicing my fear.

I shake my head. "She said someone was following her."

"Did she say what kind of car, or if she got a look at the driver?"

A deep cold settles in my chest. "She said Tatum's name."

Prescott frowns at me. "The football player?"

I drag my fingers through my hair, tugging at it. "The guy is obsessed with her, but he wouldn't hurt her." I saw what a mess he'd been when he'd hit her by accident.

Prescott heaves a heavy sigh. "Maybe it wasn't her he was trying to hurt."

"What are you talking about."

"Think about it. She was driving *your* car."

I frown at him. "You don't know this guy. I hate how close he is with Charlie, but he's not an asshole. He wouldn't..."

Prescott shrugs and we sit in silence for what seems like hours before a doctor comes in. He doesn't get a chance to speak before Jill and Daphne, followed by Tatum, come into the room, all three looking about as miserable as I feel.

"Is she okay?" Daphne asks, a little too dramatically.

"Can we see her?" Jill wrings her hands together, real concern in her eyes.

Tatum stands back, his face ashen, and Prescott's words ring through my head again. But as much as I dislike the dude, he doesn't strike me as the vengeful type. And I'm usually pretty good at reading people. What I do see when I look at him is grief.

"Are you family?" the doctor asks, looking displeased by the sudden intrusion.

I'm not exactly happy about them being here either, but I'm more concerned about Charlie.

"Just tell us. How is she?" I demand, standing and meeting the man's beady eyes. I'm pretty sure Prescott already played the money card at the front desk, because the man just swallows and nods.

"She suffered a concussion, and there was some damage to her spleen, but she's stable now and currently in the ICU."

I let out the breath I was holding in. "Take me to her."

"Our policy only allows—"

"My family donated six million to your research program last year alone, so unless you want to be the one responsible for losing future funding, I suggest you take me to her now."

The man winces but gives a small nod and motions for me to follow him.

She's all right, I say over and over in my head as we walk down the corridor and through a few sets of automatic doors.

I don't know what to expect, especially when we pass other rooms with patients hooked up to machines helping them breathe, tubes and wires everywhere. But I feel like my heart starts beating again when I turn the corner of the small room and see Charlie sitting up in bed, a smile spreading across her lips when her gaze lands on me.

She lets out a small cry as I remove the distance between us and wrap my arms around her.

"Ouch. Careful."

"Shit." I pull back, realizing I was leaning on her IV. "Sorry." Cupping her jaw, I kiss her softly. "You scared the shit out of me."

She lets out a small laugh. "I scared myself. But the doctor said I'm going to be all right."

I take her in, the small gauze bandage on her forehead, the monitors that are attached to her chest.

"He said something about your spleen?"

She winces and gingerly places her hand on her side. "Something dug into me. I think they said twenty-four stitches. But I'm in a lot better shape than your car. God, I'm so sorry—"

I tangle my fingers in her hair and kiss her forehead, her nose, her lips. "I can buy another car. There'll never be another Charlotte Hayes."

"I love you," she breathes out.

"You have no idea how much I love you," I tell her. "Do you remember what happened?"

Her mouth tugs down. "Everything is still so blurry. I was talking to you, and there was a car..."

"Did you see the make or model?"

She licks her lips and nods slowly.

"Charlie?" I place my thumb under her chin and lift her face to me when she looks away. My chest squeezes in warning, but I demand, "Tell me."

"It was a Taurus. I don't know what color, because it was dark."

My nostrils flare, and I try to hold back the anger that starts to bubble inside, because I know that's the exact make and model that Tatum drives.

"And the driver? Did you see him?" I can tell she wants to hold something back. "Charlie. If it's someone you know, it could be the same person who sent you the notes and vandalized your dorm."

"I know," she says weakly.

"It's not just you the person has hurt, it's also Ava," I say, knowing she won't tell me unless I make this not just about her. "If you saw them—"

"It was a guy..." She blinks and a tear runs down her cheek. "After the accident, he stopped and got out of the car. I didn't see his face, but..." Her bottom lip trembles and she closes her eyes for a brief moment. "He had on a Princeton Athletics sweatshirt. It had a stain on the back..."

"Okay," I say, trying to remain calm, and get as much information from her as possible. "What else?"

"I caused it."

"What?"

She blinks and shakes her head. "Bleach. I accidentally dropped some on the sweatshirt when I was washing it."

"I don't understand." But then it hits me - she used to do Tatum's laundry.

Fuck. I didn't want to believe it. Not really. But there's no denying the truth now. Fury burns so hot that I'm surprised my entire body doesn't combust from it. I'll kill the motherfucker. Even if he didn't know she was the one driving, he still put Charlie at risk.

I kiss her forehead again. "I'll deal with it. Everything is going to be okay."

"Tatum," she says on a gasp.

At first, I think she's admitting that it was him who caused the accident, but then I follow her gaze. Glancing over my shoulder, I see the bastard hovering in the doorway.

"Sorry," he mutters. "I know I shouldn't be

here, but I wanted to make sure—"

He doesn't get the last words out, because I have him by the collar of his jacket and slammed up against the wall. The guy is bigger than me, but he doesn't have the adrenaline rushing through his veins that I do in this moment. And when I slam my fist into his face, he doesn't even try to stop me.

"What the hell is that for?" Tatum spits out.

"Get the fuck out of here. And I swear to God I will kill you if you ever go near her again."

He has the nerve to look at me like I've lost my mind - and maybe I have. The thought of losing Charlie did something to me tonight.

"Spencer," Charlie says softly behind me, but I'm fixated on the asshole who almost killed her.

"You won't get away with this. Any of it. Once my lawyers are done with you, you'll be lucky to get out of prison before—"

"Jesus, Beckett. You're insane. What are you talking about?"

I'm about to slam my fist in his face again, but alarms start going off around me. There's a split second of disorientation before I realize that they're coming from Charlie's machine.

When I glance back at the bed, her eyes are closed and her face has gone ashen. I move to the side of the bed and take her face in my hands, but she doesn't respond. "Charlie? No. Don't do this. Please, please, please. Wake up, sweetheart." I press my lips to hers. Nothing, and the monitors continue to beep erratically. I turn back to Tatum whose standing like a statue. "Get some fucking help."

But before he has a chance to move, a whole team is pouring into the room. Someone pushes me aside, and there's a flurry of activity.

"Help me," I yell, trying to get back to her. "Charlie, come on...wake up sweetheart."

"Get them out of here," someone shouts.

"She's flatlining," one of the nurses says as the erratic beeping stops, followed by one high-pitched tone.

No. No. No.

This is not happening. She's fine. She was just sitting up, talking to me.

I'm yelling, but I'm not sure what the hell I'm saying, and when large hands grab me and pull me out of the room I fight like a banshee to get back to her. It isn't until I'm up against a wall, that I realize it's Tatum whose fingers dig into my shoulder.

"I need to help—"

"You can't do anything but get in the way."

I fight him, knowing that the only thing in this

world that matters is being ripped away. And there's nothing I can do.

"Get the fuck off me," I growl at Tatum. "Can't...can't lose her."

His hands drop and I see his strength drain from him. "It looks like we're both going to lose her," he tells me, his own eyes filled with tears as we both hear the long monotone beep that comes from the other room.

It's the sound of my own heart shattering across the floor of this cold and sterile hospital room.

It's the sound of the woman I love, dying. She isn't even in my arms, where she belongs.

It's the sound of our happily-ever-after being ripped away from us, one last time.

PRINCETON CHARMING SERIES

Kissing Princeton Charming

Dating Princeton Charming

Losing Princeton Charming

Forever Princeton Charming

C.M. SEABROOK

Amazon bestselling author C.M. Seabrook writes hot, steamy romances with possessive bad boys, and the passionate, fiery women who love them. Swoon-worthy romances from the heart!

For something a little different, read Chantel Seabrook's Shifter, Reverse Harem, and Fantasy books here https://amzn.to/2MTiItI

SIGN UP FOR C.M. Seabrook's NEWSLETTER FOR LATEST NEWS!
Copy and paste the following link: http://eepurl.com/cB56an

Join her FB group for giveaways and more!
www.facebook.com/groups/cmseabrook/

She loves to hear from her readers and can be reached at cm.seabrook.books@gmail.com

ALSO BY C.M. SEABROOK

Men with Wood Series

Second Draft

Second Shot

Fighting Blind Series

Theo

Moody

Wild Irish Series

Wild Irish

Tempting Irish

Taming Irish

Savages & Saints Series

Torment

Gravity

Salvage

Beast

Standalones

Melting Steel

FRANKIE LOVE

Frankie Love writes sexy stories about bad boys and mountain men. As a thirty-something mom who is ridiculously in love with her own bearded hottie, she believes in love-at-first-sight and happily-ever-afters. She also believes in the power of a quickie.

> Find Frankie here:
> *www.frankielove.net*
> *frankieloveromance@gmail.com*

JOIN FRANKIE LOVE'S MAILING LIST

AND NEVER MISS A RELEASE!

ALSO BY FRANKIE LOVE

The Mountain Man's Babies

TIMBER

BUCKED

WILDER

HONORED

CHERISHED

BUILT

CHISELED

HOMEWARD

SIX MEN OF ALASKA

The Wife Lottery

The Wife Protectors

The Wife Gamble

The Wife Code

The Wife Pact

The Wife Legacy

MOUNTAIN MEN OF LINESWORTH

MOUNTAIN MAN CANDY

MOUNTAIN MAN CAKE

MOUNTAIN MAN BUN

#OBSESSED

MOUNTAIN MEN OF BEAR VALLEY

Untamed Virgins

Untamed Lovers

Untamed Daddy

Untamed Fiance

Stand-Alone Romance

B.I.L.F.

BEAUTY AND THE MOUNTAIN MAN

HIS Everything

HIS BILLION DOLLAR SECRET BABY

UNTAMED

RUGGED

HIS MAKE BELIEVE BRIDE

HIS KINKY VIRGIN

WILD AND TRUE

BIG BAD WOLF

MISTLETOE MOUNTAIN: A MOUNTAIN MAN'S CHRISTMAS

Our Virgin

Protecting Our Virgin

Craving Our Virgin

Forever Our Virgin

F*ck Club

A-List F*ck Club

Small Town F*ck Club

Modern-Mail Order Brides

CLAIMED BY THE MOUNTAIN MAN

ORDERED BY THE MOUNTAIN MAN

WIFED BY THE MOUNTAIN MAN

EXPLORED BY THE MOUNTAIN MAN

CROWN ME

COURTED BY THE MOUNTAIN PRINCE

CHARMED BY THE MOUNTAIN PRINCE

CROWNED BY THE MOUNTAIN PRINCE

CROWN ME, PRINCE: The Complete Collection

Las Vegas Bad Boys

ACE

KING

MCQUEEN

JACK

Los Angeles Bad Boys

COLD HARD CASH

HOLLYWOOD HOLDEN

SAINT JUDE

THE COMPLETE COLLECTION

Made in the USA
Middletown, DE
06 April 2019